ALPHA'S PREY

A BBW BEAR SHIFTER ROMANCE

RENEE ROSE
LEE SAVINO

Published in the United States of America

Renee Rose Romance, Silverwood Press and Midnight Romance, LLC

Editor: Maggie Ryan

This book is a work of fiction. While reference might be made to actual historical events or existing locations, the names, characters, places and incidents are either the product of the authors' imaginations or are used fictiously, and any resemblance to actual persons, living or dead, business establishments, events, or locales is entirely coincidental.

This book contains descriptions of many BDSM and sexual practices, but this is a work of fiction and, as such, should not be used in any way as a guide. The author and publisher will not be responsible for any loss, harm, injury, or death resulting from use of the information contained within. In other words, don't try this at home, folks!

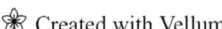 Created with Vellum

WANT FREE BOOKS?

ACKNOWLEDGMENTS

A huge thank you to Aubrey Cara, who is without a doubt, the best beta reader on Earth and to Maggie Ryan, the best editor on Earth.

Thank you to the members of Lee's Goddess Group and Renee's Romper Room for your support and love (if you're not a member and you're in Facebook, please join!). Thanks to our ARC readers and to Ardent Prose PR and the bloggers who support our releases. You are all amazing!

CHAPTER 1

*aleb*

SNOW CRUNCHES UNDER MY BOOTS. I shake my head to clear the metallic scent of blood from my nose.

I'm going fucking nuts.

No. Something evil lurks in these woods. It drew me out of my cabin this afternoon, sent me hiking through the brush.

It's a prickle at the back of my neck.

The imagined scent of evil in my nostrils. I know the scent isn't real because no matter how hard I look, I find nothing.

No mauled bodies left torn at the river's edge. No screams of my mate and cub.

It could just be a figment of my memory...the nightmare. From the trauma of their still unexplained death three years ago. From spending too much time in bear form since then. I'm more beast than man these days, and I know it shows.

I heard the wolves in Tucson mutter about me when I was there for a fight last month.

That bear should've been put down after he lost his mate. He's going to hurt somebody one of these days.

It's true.

Leaving my winter hibernation to go to Arizona and fight that grizzly was stupid. I should never have let the idiot wolf Trey talk me into it. I should be holed up in my cabin for the winter. But he knew just how to poke the bear. He insinuated something dark about the grizzly I was going to fight, and damn if it didn't make me have to go sniff the asshole myself.

Just in case he's the bear who killed my family.

He wasn't. He was an ordinary grizzly shifter. Rough, like most bears, but not wrong. Not evil.

But at least I came home with the money from the fight. I was flat broke before it. I gave most of my earnings from summer construction to one of my co-workers whose little boy needed surgery, and the rest of it had dwindled. That's the shit-can of taking winters off.

So I roused myself. Drove to the desert. Made enough money to keep me in blueberries and salmon for eight months.

But now I can't settle back in. I'm out here letting my dick swing in the wind as I hike restlessly through the forest.

Another woman's gone missing.

That's part of why I can't rest.

There's a serial killer, or kidnapper, loose up here.

I reach the main road sooner than expected. I walked three miles across my land without noticing. A blue Subaru pulls around the bend. I don't recognize it, which is strange. I know most all the cars that come and go over this road, at least during winter. I stare into the SUV as it passes me, and when I see who's driving, give a low curse.

A single female. A curvy redhead with a don't-fuck-with-me look on her face. Alone, with suitcases in her car.

Shit.

The prickles on the back of my neck grow stronger.

I know where she's going. She's headed to the University of New Mexico research station. It's a small cabin ten miles out on U.S. Forest road.

I wouldn't give a shit except three single females have disappeared from this forest in the last eight months.

Three.

And I consider this to be my fucking forest. I'm the apex predator. No other creature—beast or human—should be bringing down humans.

Especially females.

I'm not charming or chivalrous, and I sure as hell have never been known as a gentleman, but protecting females is hard-wired into me.

I skirt along the ridge, watching her car. She pulls in and parks at the only convenience store in our tiny town.

Goddammit.

Looks like I'll be spending the next week playing bodyguard to the determined researcher. The one too stupid to know not to come here in March. Alone.

Especially when there's a serial killer on the loose.

~

Miranda

I PULL in at the roadside market in Pecos to get supplies for the week.

I didn't plan on coming up here again until late spring, but my tree ring research couldn't wait. I have a paper to publish by June and to meet that deadline, I need the numbers now.

Dr. Alogore's voice still rings in my head. *"Another delay, and you lose funding. Get the numbers, now."*

When I argued that it was March, still winter in our Sangre de Cristo mountains, the southernmost tip of the Rockies, and—

"I don't see your fellow researchers asking for the same type of special treatment for their projects."

My cheeks heat as he smirks at me. Around the table my fellow researchers, all male, smirk with him. I don't need to look around to know they're all laughing internally at me. They mirror everything Dr. Alogore says or does. They even wear what he wears—right down to the fashion offensive plaid tie and brown Dockers.

"Fine," I mutter, dropping my eyes to my yellow folder. It's a bright spot of color in a drab room, and I chose it to give me a spark of joy in my otherwise weary day. But today it's just yellow, the color of cowards.

"That's it, sweetheart," Dr. Alogore says to my blouse. I want to put my hand to my neckline, but stop myself in time. I feel the gaze of all my male colleagues resting on

my modest sweater set. My grandma dresses less conservatively than I do, but I still get leers like I'm in lingerie. The way these guys look at me, I feel like they're imagining me naked. Maybe they are. Yeah, I have big breasts. The rest of me is pretty curvy too. That doesn't mean I should be treated any differently.

"If that's all, let's head out to lunch. My treat," the professor says. Everyone murmurs gratefully except me. Dr. Alogore prefers lunch joints where the women dance on tables.

I grab my folder and scurry into the hall.

"Hey, Miranda," one of my tall colleagues separates himself from the Dockers-wearing pack and comes to breathe down my neck. I turn and get a faceful of onion breath. He smiles like a shark, his eyes on my chest. "I'll come up and help you collect that data."

Ew.

"No, thank you," I mutter and pull my cardigan closed. I'm not even baring cleavage. These guys are just creepers.

"Come on. I can help. It's scary up there in the mountains this time of year," he says with false concern. "We go up there together, and I can help you grab everything in record time. You can buy me dinner afterwards, to thank me." His grin gets bigger. "I can help you with the findings, and we'll split the credit, half and half."

And there it is. A blatant grab for my research.

"Ugh, no thank you." I hunch my shoulders and hug the folder to my front. "What, you think you can swoop in at the last minute and I'll let you put your name above mine on the paper?"

He shrugs. "Makes sense, alphabetically—"

"No. I got this." I duck my head and walk as fast as my legs can carry me. No one is cheating me out of my research. Not this time.

This paper could make the difference between another shitty year as a postdoc in Dr. Alogore's lab and getting an actual professorial position somewhere. Anywhere. Of course, a professor position still won't guarantee me respect in my field. I've seen enough women in science have their careers belittled on a daily basis to know I'll be fighting for my equal rights every step of the way. Probably until the day I retire.

Never give up, never give in. That's my motto.

I get out in Pecos and grab my empty canvas shopping bags to fill. Inside, I blink as my eyes adjust to the dimly lit, somewhat depressing market. I've been here before, so I know what to expect, but it still makes my skin crawl. Unswept concrete floors, ancient canned goods with old-fashioned price tags. Like any convenience market near an entry to a U.S. Forest, it carries extremely overpriced gas station fare. Loaves of Wonder Bread for almost five bucks, eight dollar jars of peanut butter.

I packed my own non-perishables in Albuquerque, so I head to the refrigerator case to grab a jug of milk, some eggs, bacon, and butter. That should be enough to get me by for the five days I plan to be up here.

I bring them up to the counter where an ancient man is talking to a local. He ignores me for a solid two minutes before he slowly drags the eggs toward the register while still gabbing away.

I clear my throat.

His companion, equally old, says goodbye and shuffles out. The owner turns and eyes me speculatively. Yes, his eyes drop to my cleavage. "What brings you up here, young lady? Isn't the right time of year for fishing or hiking."

"I'm headed to the research lab for a few days," I say politely. It's the exact same conversation we had last time I was here. Granted, that was six months ago, but still. I doubt they get a ton of women camping or hiking alone.

"Oh right, right. University of New Mexico, aren't you?"

"Yes."

He stops punching numbers into the cash register and squints at me. "You be careful up there alone. You've heard about the missing women?"

I push away the dread that ripples through me. The only thing to fear is fear itself. Right?

"I've heard, yes. But I've got my dog with me. And he's very protective."

That may or may not be true. I have a furry German / Australian Shepherd mix who loves to play fetch. But he does have a ferocious-sounding bark.

"Well, you might have to protect your dog. You do know we have a bear problem in this forest, don't you?"

Right, the bear problem. He told me about it the last time I was up here. As an ecologist, I rather dislike when humans presume the animals are the problem. Wouldn't our overpopulation and the shrinkage of wildlife corridors be the actual problem?

When I was here this past summer, he leaned on the counter and squinted at me. "You be careful up here.

There's a rabid bear roaming this wilderness. Tore a woman and her child to pieces a few years back."

"If he was rabid a few years ago, he'd be dead by now, don't you think?" I hated to use science and logic as a weapon, but...please.

"Well, he may not be rabid, but he's definitely feral," the old man had claimed.

I couldn't help the scorn that must've crept over my face. "Bears can't be feral. We don't keep them as pets."

The man thumped my change down on the counter and glared at me. "Crazy, then! There's a crazy bear out there. Uncanny-like. Enormous animal with eyes that glow yellow and a real desire to destroy things. Same time that woman and her child got killed, the bear scored every tree in a three mile radius with his claws."

"Yes, yes, I've heard about your bear," I tell him now. "But you haven't had any bear problems recently, right?"

"No, it's been a few years. But something was wrong with the animal, I'm telling you. You mind your dog, or that bear might kill him just for sport—mark my words."

Right. And Bigfoot might invite me to a tea party. I wanted to argue that bear attacks are incredibly rare, and just because an animal is an apex predator doesn't mean it's out to get humans. Most animals just want to be left alone in their natural habitat. And don't get me started on the villainizing of sharks and bears and wolves in animated children's movies.

The guy points at the number on the register. "Twenty-eight twenty-two."

Yeah, like I said—overpriced.

I hand over my money and try to quell the stirring in

8

my stomach. "Okay, I'll keep him close at all times. Thanks for the warning."

Despite the fact that I'd put my reusable bags on the counter with the food, the guy slid all my food into plastic ones.

I take them and dump the food into my canvas sacks and hand the bags back to him. "I don't need these, thanks."

As I head out the door, I hear him call after me, "You be careful, you hear?"

"Yep, I will. Thank you!"

Inside my Subaru, Bear gives a happy bark to see me return.

I open the door and put the bags of groceries on the passenger seat while Bear lunges forward and tries to kiss my face from the back seat. "You ready to go to the cabin, boy?"

He chuffs and tries to lick some more.

I angle my face away and give him a quick head rub. "Go lie down," I tell him.

He promptly hops over the back seat into the trunk area, where I put his bed, and curls into it.

I smile into the rear view mirror. "Good boy."

Snowflakes hit my windshield, and I say a prayer to the weather gods. The weather app I checked said there'd be a light wintry mix but would clear up tomorrow. It will be chilly, but I should be able to complete my research and get home by the end of the week.

CHAPTER 2

aleb

IT'S SNOWING.

All I can think about is the redhead and whether she made it to her cabin safely. I feel a cold front coming in, and my bear's telling me it's gonna be a bad snowstorm. Weather turns quickly up here.

The good thing about the snow is it might deter the psycho who preys on female hikers.

The bad thing is it makes the determined researcher far more vulnerable. If she's snowed in there, she'll have nowhere to run.

Stupid, headstrong female.

No, not stupid. She's a scientist. Probably extremely smart.

But I push back my grudging admiration of sturdy, self-sufficient woman like her.

I consider the danger she might be in. There's something out there that stalks pretty young women.

Doubtful it's the same fuck who killed my family, but I'm after him, just the same. Because I know what it's like to have someone you love taken from you. And I won't stand by and let that tragedy befall others.

Not in my woods.

He must live somewhere close. Trouble is, I know everyone in town. And I think my instincts would tell me if there was someone off in Pecos. Plus, I would recognize the scent. You can't fool my nose. A bear's sense of smell is 2100 times better than a human's. Seven times better than the best bloodhound. And I remember the smell that mingled with blood and death on my family. It wasn't bear. It wasn't human, either.

It wasn't any kind of animal scent I recognize.

And maybe this is a lead, maybe it's not, but I caught the scent of something similar in Tucson. Not the same—hell, it if had been the same, the guy would be dead. But there were a few guys at the Fight Club. They were shifters, but I couldn't figure out what animal.

And that doesn't make sense.

But I didn't trust my senses when I was there. And being around all those shifters, being in the city—if you can call Tucson a city, and I do—had my bear so on edge, I was slipping between human and animal form the whole time I was there. Barely keeping my mind intact. It made me cranky as hell, and a danger to all those around me. All I wanted to do was get back on I-10 and drive away as fast as I could.

It's only here, back at my cabin where I can be the

antisocial hermit I am, I've sorted through my impressions. Now I wish I had stayed and asked questions about that scent.

I stand in my open doorway and stare out at the snow falling. Looks like going back into hibernation isn't going to be an option. I have to go check on the human.

I'm not going to drive up to the research cabin—that would only scare the shit out of her. She'd think *I'm* the psycho stalker. I'm sure she's been warned about the danger. It's getting too cold to walk now, though. At least in human form.

I could wait until morning and hike over.

My bear rumbles.

Fuck.

Looks like we're going for a four-legged hike.

I strip out of my clothes and stow them just inside the door. Outside, it's started to snow harder. The flakes stings my bare skin and the soles of my feet as I shut the door in human form. Then I close my eyes and drop to all fours, the bear always so close to the surface, ready to take over.

He runs.

He fucking loves to run.

If he had his way, I'd give up all humanity. Roam these woods as bear. Forget all the pain, the tragedy. The life hardly worth living.

I almost gave into him in the months after Jen and Gretchen died. I wanted to. I hoped he'd swallow every last bit of Caleb, leave me without the ability to go back.

But the wolves intervened. I don't know how they got word, but the Tucson wolf pack showed up on their bikes, scaring the snot out of the inhabitants of Pecos, who thought the Hell's Angels had invaded.

They hunted me as a pack. Cornered me in a fight. They're lucky I didn't kill them all. The wolves kept me cornered and Garrett Green, their alpha, took his human form and ordered me to shift. He carried enough alpha command to make me do it.

They dragged me back to my cabin and stayed with me until I was human again. Forced me back to human form every time I tried to shift.

I guess they think I ought to be grateful.

I'm not.

I hate the fuckers.

They brought me back into my pain. Into a life I don't want to lead.

On the other hand, there is something about knowing an entire pack of shifters have my back. Bears are generally solitary animals, so it was strange to be claimed by a pack. I still don't know why they did it.

Because they could've just as easily come up here and put me down.

They probably should have.

I lope through the snow, my bear chuffing with pleasure at the snow on my snout, the taste of it on my tongue, the crisp air cooling my furry ears.

The trip to the research cabin takes no time at all with my giant bear stride.

I circle it twice, getting a sense for the scents.

There's animal—dog.

That's good. I'm glad she's not entirely alone.

And the female's scent.

It's a pleasant tickle in my nose. Like strawberries and vanilla ice cream, only not that sweet. I don't expect to enjoy it so much. It's a human scent, after all. Not my thing.

The dog starts to bark when I get closer to the cabin. Smart animal.

The alpha in me growls, like I want to put him in his place, but he's doing his job. Protecting his human as he should.

I amble toward the back of the cabin. I probably don't need to stay any longer. I don't detect any other scents here. But something pulls me closer. Some idle curiosity about the fearless female who thinks coming up here alone in a snowstorm with a killer on the loose is a good plan.

I stand on my hind legs and put my paws on the windowsill, peering in.

Fuck. *Me.*

The girl—scratch that, she's all woman, even though she's young—has built too big a fire. I know it's too big because she's stripped down to a soft pink tank top. A *very small* soft pink tank top. One that strains to contain her large, lush breasts. A pretty tattoo winds around her upper arm—green vines and a cobalt blue butterfly.

My bear growls.

She's fucking beautiful. Human females aren't my type —not at all. But if they were, I'd pick her kind. She looks like a Swiss milkmaid. A Viking princess. No, with that red hair, she'd be Irish farmstock. She's sturdy. Big-boned, well-padded. Full-bodied with wide enough hips to carry a bear cub. Full strawberry lips. Smooth creamy white skin.

She's healthy as fuck.

With brains to boot.

She will make some human asshole a very lucky man if she hasn't already.

The dog, a furry black shepherd of some kind goes nuts when I growl, baring his teeth and snarling toward the window.

I should turn away, but I don't. I haven't looked my fill, yet.

I'm still staring when the hot scientist whirls and catches sight of me. Her eyes fly wide and she shrieks. More of a yelp, really. Almost a battle cry. She lunges for her dog as if he might be in imminent danger and grabs him by the collar.

"Bear, stay back." She doesn't take her eyes from me.

The command tickles something in me. An inner smile. How cute that she thinks she can command a bear.

But then she repeats, *"Bear, no,"* and I realize she's talking to the dog.

Hilarious.

Miranda

Oh holy mother of God.

The guy at the store was right. There is a crazy freaking bear up here.

Because I swear to God, it's smiling at me right now. It must be nearly nine feet tall, with an intense, intelligent yellow gaze. Like it's reading my thoughts.

My heart pounds, but logic takes over. The bear's outside. Bear—my dog—and I are inside. As soon as I'm sure of it, maybe even before, my knees go weak at the sheer splendor of the animal.

I've never met a bear in person before. Sure, I've seen them behind the glass at the zoo, but this is totally different. I'm witnessing a bear in the wild.

"*Ursus americanus.* The American black bear," I say in a mock deep voice like a narrator of a nature documentary—it's one of my favorite games. A party trick I developed as an undergrad for laughs. "Named for its black fur, although the species' coat can have variations of brown or blonde." And this one is absolutely magnificent. He's a black bear, but the size of a grizzly. Healthy—with a shiny thick coat of dark fur.

I continue lecturing my imaginary audience, "In the cold months, the bear's metabolism slows to the point where the bear can enter a dormant state known as hibernation. The bear can conserve energy and weather the season when food is scarce."

Why on Earth is he not still hibernating? We did have a brief warm spell; maybe it pulled him out of his cave early.

Poor bear. Tricked by nature.

God, I hope he can survive. What will he find to eat when the rivers are half frozen and nothing's in bloom?

Well, I suppose that's why he's roaming around this cabin. Probably smells food.

Of course, I can't feed him. That's a terribly dangerous proposition, and it teaches bears to associate humans with food, which leads to bear attacks.

Maybe I can leave something out in the woods when

I'm doing my research. But it will still smell like a human. And I recall that bears have an excellent sense of smell—300 times better than a dog or something crazy like that.

Too bad they can't train a bear to hunt and seek. Maybe they'd find the women who have disappeared.

The bear tips his head to the side, eyes locked onto mine like he's trying to read my mind. A tingle races across my skin. Now I see why the townspeople think the bear is crazy. There is something uncanny about it. It seems to have an almost human intelligence.

"Hey, big guy," I murmur. "You're beautiful." Bear stops growling, following my lead. He sits but keeps his gaze pinned to the real bear in the window, ears cocked forward, haunches bunched and ready to spring into action.

The giant bear chuffs, fogging the glass.

I smile. I can't help it. I feel so honored to catch sight of such a magnificent creature. As often happens in the face of raw nature, I'm filled with awe—overwhelmed with appreciation for the incredible beauty and largess of everything this Earth has to hold.

It's why I became an ecologist. And I'm grateful for moments like these that remind me. This is what I need to remember when I'm overwhelmed by the sexism and insularity of academia.

When I was an undergrad, I spent a summer volunteering in Guatemala. My job was to build latrines. While I was there I felt an earthquake. Nothing huge. Just a tremor, or *temblor* as they called it. But in that moment I felt so helpless. I realized how tiny and insignificant humans are in the face of natural forces. It didn't scare me—it humbled me. Renewed my respect for Mother Earth and all she represents.

It's unwise—not because I'm in danger, but because I shouldn't let this bear get comfortable around humans—but I step forward to get a closer look. To indulge my awe.

The bear chuffs again but doesn't move. I advance slowly, taking in every detail of the beautiful creature. The unblinking golden gaze, the tan coloring around his snout.

"You are gorgeous aren't you?" I croon.

I swear the bear smiles again, but then he drops away from view. I dash to the window and peer out as he lopes away. It's insane how much territory he covers with just a few bounds, his powerful legs eating up ground like he owns it.

I guess he does. The bears should own these mountains. They shouldn't be pushed out of their natural wilderness by the growing competition for space.

I hum softly to myself as I watch him grow smaller and then disappear into the falling snow and settling dusk. There's a lot more snow than I expected—the weather app was wrong.

Lucky me. A giant black bear sighting. I've never seen New Mexico's state animal before. I mean, outside of a zoo. That alone makes the entire trip worth it. Not that I don't love coming up to this cabin. Spending time alone in nature is my favorite thing—even in the winter. I sort of love the solitary rustic cabin in the woods thing. I've been applying for research grants, dreaming that the department will let me take the money and just live up here, collect and analyze data for weeks or even months at a time.

From the time I first went camping as a kid, I knew the

wilderness was where I belonged. I ended up getting my doctorate in ecology because I care deeply about nature, and I've developed a passion to protect it.

If I can prove climate change effects on the trees, it will contribute to environmental movements across the globe. That's the real reason I'm out here in the middle of a snowstorm doing research. Not for proving something to Dr. Alogore or the glory of publication. No, this is for the planet.

I'm working hard to make a difference, and I believe I will.

Caleb

I HAVE to fight to shift back to human form when I get to my cabin, and when I succeed, I have a boner the size of the Eiffel Tower.

Well.

Now I'm awake.

And it's not even spring yet.

Because I still carry the snow and dirt of the forest on my skin, I head into the shower.

As the water sluices over my body, I try not to think of that ridiculous human scientist staring at me like I'm some kind of god. The way those full lips moved around the words, *you're beautiful.*

Beautiful? Not even close.

I am darkness and despair. A formidable bear. A

pathetic man. And far too often, caught between the two—neither man nor bear, but something sick and raw and wasted.

But I can't stop the image of her from presenting itself before my eyes. Her curvy shape. The creamy skin. The very capable demeanor.

I grip my cock, trying my best not to imagine her lush mouth over it.

Oh fuck—now I thought it. And goddamn what a wonderful thought. My thighs shudder as I imagine the hot water from the shower is the heat of her mouth gliding over my length.

I probably wouldn't fit in that hot mouth of hers. Although she is ample for a human. Would she look up at me with that same glowing awe as she took me between those pouty lips? Like she wanted to worship at my feet just because I have fur and claws?

I shake my head, guilt shutting down the fantasy like the lid on a garbage can.

How could I?

I mated Jen for life. And most bears don't settle down—we're seldom monogamous. But I did.

I shouldn't be getting turned on by any other female. Especially not a human.

Except my cock disagrees. Even my bear disagrees—he's right at the surface, urging me to shift and charge back to the research cabin. I'm still rock hard, and my fist hasn't stopped moving up and down over the throbbing appendage.

Fuck.

Well, it's not like I'd actually do anything with her.

This is more like a foray into porn. I'm letting myself travel down the path of a stupid fantasy. No harm, no foul, right? I close my eyes, remembering the scent of the human female. Pleasure ripples through my body; the water's suddenly way too hot. I twist it toward cold and pump my cock harder. My balls draw up tight.

Damn, when's the last time I jacked off? It's been months. At least half a year. My body celebrates the reignition of my libido, the hormones pumping through my body. Once more, the vision of the scientist on her knees servicing me rises to the forefront of my mind.

That lush mouth…

I come, my hand jerking frantically as I spend onto the porcelain floor of the tub.

Relief makes me sag, leaning a shoulder against the cool tile. The pleasure only lasts a moment and then disgust rips through me.

What the hell is wrong with me? I shouldn't be thinking *anything* about that human female except how to keep my bear from breaking through and how to protect her from the evil that lurks in the woods.

CHAPTER 3

*M*iranda

I BUNDLE up before I head out the next morning. The snow flurries stopped, which is good, because I didn't want to wait to start my research. And I'm glad I made it up here yesterday, because the roads would probably be icy today. I'm just counting on the weather clearing after a few days so I can get home at the end of the week.

Bear stands at the door, turning in circles with excitement over going for a walk.

"You want outside, boy? You ready for our hike?" I egg him on.

He whirls again, paws prancing with readiness, furry tail wagging. I love this dog. Really—he makes my day on a regular basis.

"Okay, let's go, then." I pull on my leather gloves.

They're not as warm as big insulated mittens, but I have work to do out there, and I'll need individual fingers.

I grab my backpack which has everything I require in it: my tablet, battery pack charger, snacks for lunch and a water bottle. I bring my phone for emergencies, although reception is so bad out here, I doubt it would do any good.

As soon as I open the door, wind hits us. I gasp out loud, then laugh at my reaction. "Damn, it's cold, isn't it buddy?"

Bear charged out into the snow, rushing around to re-investigate every snow-covered bush he already sniffed and peed on when he went out this morning. He pays particular attention to the side of the cabin where the bear —the real bear—stood last night.

I wrap my scarf tighter around my face, leaving only my eyes uncovered and tucking the edges into my coat to stuff all the weak points where the wind cuts right through me. I look up at the sky. It's sunny now, but clouds are moving in from the north. I need to plan to be back to the cabin by lunchtime in case another storm comes in.

"We'll have to keep the research short today, won't we, boy?"

Bear bounds in front of me like the snow was a gift just for him.

It's easy to follow the road, even though it's covered in snow, and I know the trails well enough. Staying cooped up in the cabin all day without having research numbers to crunch doesn't sound fun. If I can at least get started today, I'll feel better.

I trudge through the accumulation, which is knee deep

in places. It hits above my boots and clings to my jeans in little ice-balls. Damn. I'm going to get too cold very fast.

Bear doesn't seem to mind. He's still bounding around, zipping ahead of me to investigate, then tunneling back through the snow.

"You'd make a good sled dog, wouldn't you, Bear? Wish I had a sled today, that would make this much easier." Or skis. Or snowshoes. This is insane.

It takes me three times longer than usual to make it to the trailhead. I push on, cutting off onto the trail and following it up on a slow ascent.

I start by setting up my plot—marking off an acre of land as my sample area. Then I begin, starting with the first giant ponderosa tree. I take a core sample to take back to the lab to examine the rings. I'm studying the effects of climate change on trees, and it's measurable. Soon I'll have enough data to prove it and finally get some credit as a researcher at the University of New Mexico.

"Observe the female of the species," I say in my documentary-narrator voice. "Relegated to home life in past centuries, breakthroughs in contraception allow her greater freedom and control of her professional life. She is able to accept duties and responsibilities equal to her male colleagues, at eighty percent of their take home pay. Perceived as the weaker sex, she endures the males' posturing and attempts at bullying as the price of entry into the workplace." At least until I secure funding for my project. Then it's "*Sayonara*, suckas!" I squeeze my fingers to warm them up, and get to work.

For the next couple of hours, I continue gathering my samples. With the snow, it's hard to stay on the trail, but

I'm fairly confident I have. It doesn't much matter—returning to the cabin will be easy. All I have to do is follow our footprints in the snow.

I'm about to stop and have a snack when the wind whips up. I didn't realize the clouds had moved in, blotting out the sun.

Damn. No time for a break. We need to get back to the cabin before the storm hits. I whistle for Bear. Wind blasts my face and cuts through my clothing. It whips around in gusts, making it unclear if it started snowing or if it's just stirring up the snow that fell yesterday.

I mutter in my David Attenborough impersonation, "Weather patterns are susceptible to great change in the mountains. Warm days—enough to wake a hibernating bear—followed by drops in temperature that precipitate winter storms—" A sharp wind cuts across my throat, and I give up the mini documentary gag. It's cold as hell. I need to get out of here.

Up ahead, I hear Bear going crazy—barking and growling at something.

"Bear! Here, boy!" I make my voice sharp with command, but Bear doesn't come running.

What in the hell is out there?

Panic smashes through me. What if it's the bear from last night?

Oh God, don't hurt my dog.

As if on cue, the wind streaks through the trees, and this time, I'm sure it's snowing. Precipitation pelts my face —hard.

I break into a run, following the sound of Bear's barks. "Bear! Come here! *Bear, come!*"

Terror races through my veins when he still doesn't come and his growls and low barks continue. I catch sight of him, only to see him tear off into the distance, like he's chasing something away.

Shit.

"Bear, no! Bad dog," I yell in my deepest, maddest voice.

He's usually an extremely obedient dog. Maybe a little spoiled, but he always comes when called. Now, though, I see snatches of him through the trees as he chases whatever he was growling at.

Damn dog.

It's not even like this is our first foray into the woods.

"Bear! Bear, come back! Now!"

Finally, he stops. In the distance, I see him turn and look in my direction, then back the way he was going.

"No! Come here!"

He gives one more long look away, then trots back to me, tail tucked, slinking a bit from the growl in my voice.

I scold him when he arrives and turn back to find the path.

Fuck.

It's snowing so hard our tracks are almost already obscured.

I start running.

"Come on, Bear. We have to move fast," I pant. The altitude up here kicks my ass on a good day, but add to it freezing air, and my lungs ache just from breathing. I push on, trying to stay one step ahead of my rising panic.

If I get lost out here, I have no way to contact anyone

for help. Bear and I will freeze to death before anyone finds us.

My feet push through the snow. I stumble on something under the powder and pitch headlong, face planting in eighteen inches of cold wet flakes. Bear trots back and licks my ear as I scramble to my feet.

No time to waste. We have to keep moving. I run even harder, which, of course, means I trip again.

And again.

Crap, I think I'm just getting clumsy from the cold.

I start running again, only to realize I just reversed directions—I'm following my fresh tracks rather than the old ones.

Holy fuck. Where are the old ones?

I spin around, panic fully gripping my throat. A pathetic whimper comes from my mouth.

"It's okay, Bear," I mutter. "We'll figure it out, won't we? Do you know which way is home?" I scan the area for anything that looks familiar, but it's all blanketed in white. I don't have a clue where we are or even which direction we came from. "Go home, Bear," I try but he just cocks his ears and wags his snow-crusted tail, not understanding me.

I attempt to take a deep breath, but my lungs reject the cold air. I can do this. I can figure this out. Downhill.

We need to head downhill, right? When we got on the trail we were on an incline, so as long as we're going downhill, we must be moving in the right direction.

Where is the river? That would help me figure out where we are.

The trouble is, it's hard to tell what's downhill and uphill right now. I can hardly see five feet in front of me.

The wind swirls at all kinds of crazy angles, pelting my face with snow. I do my best to orient myself to the mountain and pick the most logical direction. I can figure this out. If we just keep moving, eventually we'll either hit town or the river or something. And we won't freeze to death unless we stop.

It's idiotic but that *Finding Nemo* song *Just Keep Swimmin* starts playing in my head. Great—just what we needed—a theme song for this trek.

An hour later, I'm exhausted, my jeans are frozen to my legs and I'm starving. I call to Bear, stopping to pull some food out of my backpack. I eat a granola bar and feed him one, too. "We'll just rest a minute and then we'll keep going, okay, boy?" I lean my back against a tree. It feels so good to stop. Funny, but it's not that cold anymore, either.

I let myself slide down to sit. God, yes. I just need to rest for a little while. Rest and warm up here under this tree. Maybe the skies will clear up in a bit and it will be easy to find our way back.

Or the snow will melt…

Bear nudges me. Licks my face.

Then he barks.

"It's okay, boy," I mutter.

I'm suddenly so very sleepy.

I hardly notice that Bear has started to bark louder and louder…

Test Subject 849

. . .

FEMALE. Female in the woods and I lost her.

Damn dog.

We need the female for our tests. Our very important testing. We need to measure how much pain she can withstand to determine what stressors trigger the change.

No, not the change.

These females don't change.

Why don't they change?

Perhaps with the right stressor they can find their inner animal. With enough injections of the serum.

The way mine manifests in moments of extreme danger or fear.

Or partly manifests.

If I'd had enough testing, enough practice, I might have learned to control the wild animal within me. The rage. The terror.

I need to develop the serum to fix my animal. So I can fully transform.

That's why I have to help these women. Give them more tests. More trials to endure. More pain. Soon they will become the animals they long to be.

Soon we will get the results we've been working for.

∿

Caleb

. . .

THERE'S A RAGING SNOWSTORM OUTSIDE. My bear should want to hunker down and sleep, but something pulls me out of the cabin. The same bad feeling I had yesterday, but amplified. Maybe I'm just going nuts.

It's always there. That possibility. I spent too much time in bear form. My human reasoning has been affected. My self-control.

I pull open the door and a gust of wind stings my face with snow. I'm in human form, but I lift my nose to the air, anyway, sniffing. I hear something. It's faint, but a dog barks. There's a frightened timbre to the bark that I pick up, even at a distance. It's a warning bark—an emergency bark.

Fuck.

My skin itches, the urge to shift right upon me. Any sign of danger and my bear wants to rush forward. It's why I'm hardly fit for human company these days.

Right now my bear's on edge because I know exactly whose dog is barking, and I'm terrified to find out why. I dive back into the cabin and yank on my boots and a jacket and hat, then head out into the snowstorm.

"Keep barking, dog. I'm coming," I say out loud. As long as he keeps it up, I should be able to locate them. I'm hoping it's a *them* I'm rescuing and not just him.

I'm hoping it's the storm that threatens them and not something—someone—else.

My long strides turn into a run the more my mind whirls around all the things that might have gone wrong. The heat of the shift is right at the surface. I want to take my bear form so I can cover more ground, get there quicker, but I resist the urge. I won't be of much use to the lovely scientist in bear form. Not unless she's under direct attack.

The memory of finding Jen and Gretchen dead comes flooding back, and I nearly lose control.

Please, no.

Don't let that happen again.

When I get close, the dog charges, running at me, growling viciously. He stops halfway between me and her, sits and just barks. The poor beast isn't sure whether to protect his mistress from me or lead me to her. His instincts are going haywire right now with the need to survive and to help his owner.

Poor creature. I ignore him, showing my dominance. He whines as I pass, probably catching my scent and realizing I'm not human. At least not completely.

I find the young scientist slumped against a tree. Her eyes are open, but she doesn't seem terribly aware. She's probably in some stage of hypothermia.

Christ.

What the hell happened to her out here? I sniff but don't detect any scent but hers and the dog's.

As soon as she recovers from this mess, I'm going to turn her over my knee for even being out on a day like this.

Okay… that was a weird thought.

I would never do anything like that.

With any female.

…who wasn't my mate.

Lord, I've been living up here alone too long. I shouldn't be so affected by the first female who comes around. Especially when she's human.

I reach down and pluck the scientist from the ground,

tugging her to her feet first, then bending and slinging her over my shoulder.

She mumbles something incoherent, but I ignore it. The danger isn't over and I still have to get her back to my cabin and warmed up. I would run, but I'm afraid it would jostle her too much. I don't want to snap the fragile human's neck. I settle for long, hurried strides.

The dog runs along beside me, trying to jump up and lick his master's face.

We reach my cabin and even though I don't keep the gas heaters turned up, warmth seems to blast us.

The human whimpers as I tip her to her feet. It occurs to me I ought to say something to her, something reassuring, but those kind of words are long forgotten. I hardly speak to anyone these days, and when I do, it's not pleasantries. I don't do polite. Or chit chat. Definitely not friendly.

Soothing is so far out of my wheelhouse it's in the next kingdom.

I pull off her backpack and dump it behind the door. "Come here," I grunt, taking her elbow and propelling her to my bathroom. She stands there, disoriented and docile as I fill the tub with tepid water.

I shuck her soaked leather gloves from her hands, then unzip her jacket and tug it off. Her eyes widen slightly, but she seems incapable of speech just yet.

"Gotta get your body temperature up," I growl, peeling her sweater off next, then the sexy pink tank top I saw her in last night.

Her bra is also pink, and as much as I try not to look at her tits, I'm fucking dazzled by them when they tumble

33

out. They're big and bouncy. Creamy white with a smattering of copper freckles across the tops and between them.

The nipples—fuck, the nipples are perfection. A rosy-peach and harder than glass.

She has the wherewithal to cover her breasts—at least she tries, but her fingers aren't working yet, so she holds them loosely in front of her face, like her fingers are broken, and uses her forearms to cover the nips.

After taking off her boots, I unbutton her jeans. She just stands there and lets me. I don't know why the fuck she didn't have snow pants on if she was going out in this blizzard.

I don't know why the fuck she went out in this blizzard at all, but I intend to find out.

Later.

When she can speak.

Her jeans are frozen to her legs. I wince peeling them off her chafed red skin. I hope to fates she didn't get frostbite.

"W-who are you?" she manages to say as I steady her hips and pull off her socks. Thank fuck they're wool. Toes still look intact.

"I'm the guy who saved you from freezing to death." It's a shitty answer, but grouchy is my M.O.

When I try to pull down her panties—cotton, also pale pink—she catches them, or at least tries to.

"Fine," I snap. "Leave them on." I lift my chin toward the tub. "You're getting in there."

I steady her elbow and direct her into the bath. She yelps in pain when her foot comes in contact with the warm water. I was careful not to make it too warm, but I'm sure it still burns like hell.

"I know. It's gonna hurt when the blood comes back into the area. Take it slow." *There.* I can be somewhat civil.

She grits her teeth and leans on me to step her other foot in, sucking her breath in across her teeth.

"Now sit down in it. I have to deal with your dog."

Her eyes fly wide. "Bear? Where's Bear?" She tries to peer around me, which is cute, because I'm way too big to see past.

Her dog's right behind me—totally underfoot. He gives a soft whine when he hears his name.

"Is he okay?"

My bear likes that she's more worried about her dog than herself, but I'm not surprised. I already got the impression they're tight. And that she's an animal lover.

"He saved your fucking life," I tell her.

"That's not what I asked." Her teeth chatter as she lowers herself into the tub, crying out when her butt hits the water.

"I don't know. I'm trying to get your ass thawed out first."

"Charming," she mutters, gasping and wincing as she sinks in deeper.

As soon as I'm sure she's not going to drown or anything, I grab a towel and throw it over her dog. It doesn't do much good, because his thick fur is matted with ice and snow, which isn't yet melted.

Fuck.

Somewhere, I think I have a hairdryer. It was Jen's, but

I kept it because it comes in handy on occasion. Not for hair, but for fix-it projects, like drying glue or wet plaster. I find it under the sink and plug it in.

"Dog," I say sternly. The dog cowers.

"Why is my dog scared of you?"

I glance her way. She still appears shell-shocked. Barely alive. Confused. It irritates the fuck out of me because it's clear how close she came to dying. If I hadn't heard her damn dog...

I glance down at the reason she's still breathing. He tucks his tail and drops his head submissively. "Because he recognizes me as alpha," I say. *And as a giant fucking black bear.* Poor dog must be scared as hell, knowing on some level what I am.

I turn on the hairdryer, which discourages further questions. The dog stands there and takes it, hunching against the noise and blast of hot air. I keep it up until the snow has melted off him and his wet fur stinks up the bathroom.

It takes all my effort to avoid looking over at the naked scientist in my tub. In fact, I'm not even sure why I stayed in the same room with her. My concentration is being sorely tested. I should *not* be ogling her full breasts when her well-being still hangs on the line. Especially because it brings my ever-present bear even closer to the surface. Shit —my eyes are probably glowing yellow right now.

And then I do look over, because, yeah—beautiful breasts—and I realize she's not recovering as quickly as I'd expected.

Of course, I know dick about human females, but I didn't expect her teeth to still be chattering, or her body to be shaking so much.

Fuck.

My bear snarls as if Death is some real foe it can defend her against. I shove him down—I can't fucking think if I'm half-crazed with animal thoughts, and I need to think. I have to figure out how to save this female.

I abandon the dog—his fur is close to dry now anyway —and march over to the tub.

"Out," I order.

She doesn't move. Not even her eyes. It's like she's in shock.

Damn.

I grasp behind both her elbows and lift her to stand. "Out you come," I attempt to order again. I need her help or I'll have to resort to tossing her over my shoulder again.

She just stands there, shuddering.

Dammit. I grab a towel and wrap it around her shoulders, then scoop under her knees and swoop her up into a baby carry. "Let's go, princess. Gotta get you warm."

"I'm c-c-c-cold," she chatters.

"I noticed," I say drily, carrying her out to the living room, dog at my heels. I lay her down on the couch and finish toweling her off, patting the skin that's bright red from the elements gently. Her damp dog sits beside the couch, watching everything. Still alert in case she needs help.

And she does. This human needs medical attention. A hospital, or some other kind of emergency help. I don't fucking know, because shifters heal on their own without a doctor's interference.

A sleeping bag!

That's what I need.

I remember hearing it's one way to raise a person's body heat. You zip them up in a sleeping back with another body. Uh, preferably naked.

Shit. *I am so screwed.*

My cock gets hard just thinking about lying skin to skin with the lovely scientist. My bear twists just under my skin, antsy. Always antsy. Always ready to come screaming out and tear his claws and teeth into something.

Especially for a threatened female.

She's not even a bear, I want to tell him. *Calm the fuck down.*

Maybe he's lost reason, too. We've both gone mad. Me with too much time in animal form. My animal with too much… fuck if I know. Misery? Grief?

I cover the freezing female with a blanket, cursing myself for not having something softer. After I build up a roaring fire in the fireplace, I dig a sleeping bag out of the closet and drop it on the throw rug in front of the hearth. My bear's still flickering at the surface, jumbling my thoughts with deadly aggression. There's a reason people fear the mama-bear. The instinct to protect runs fierce in our species.

No one to kill here, fucker. And you'll hurt the girl if you don't back the hell down.

The human still shivers on my couch, teeth chattering. Delicate fucking flower. "Come here," I say gruffly, grasping her wrists and pulling her to stand. "We have to get your body temperature up. Get in that sleeping bag there." I point to it and lead her over.

She moves like an awkward wooden doll, her steps

stiff and uncoordinated. She manages to fit herself into the sleeping bag.

"Take off the panties."

Damn. That doesn't sound good.

She doesn't move.

"They're wet and cold. Take the damn things off now," I bark, putting alpha command into my voice. The dog hears it and tucks his tail even more, dropping his head.

I actually don't expect her to obey me. She's not a shifter so she doesn't respond to alpha command for one thing. For another, she doesn't know me at all. I'm a complete stranger ordering her to take off her panties. It could definitely be misconstrued.

After a couple beats, she wriggles around in the sleeping bag, but the movements seem to exhaust her and she falls still, just shivering.

Shit. I unzip the side of the sleeping bag and grab the sides of her panties. Her eyes fly wide when I pull them down.

I nearly shift right there. And it's not to protect her.

Apparently my bear thinks this curvy human is the next best thing to a sow because my teeth sharpen in my mouth like he wants to give her a mating bite.

Crazy, crazy bear. I need to get this under control or I could inadvertently hurt this fragile human. I close my eyes and turn my face away in case my irises turned yellow. I fight back a growl from my bear. Fates, having a naked female within kissing distance does all kinds of things to the beast within.

Go back to sleep, bear.

Touching her, lying next to her naked body is the last

thing I should do considering how little control I have over my animal. But it has to be done. Her life is still in danger.

I strip off all but my boxers, wedge myself in with her, and zip us in together. Her scent fills my nostrils—sun-warmed strawberries. Vanilla ice cream. Heat explodes down my limbs. I struggle to calm the bear, taking slow, measured breaths, focusing on the chill of her flesh against my burning skin.

I turn her to face away from me and mold myself to her back. She stiffens but doesn't protest. I pray my intent is pretty clear—this isn't a romantic moment, it's a life-saving event.

At least I hope to hell it saves her life.

Her ample ass fills my lap. Her *bare* lush ass. Nothing between it and my cock but a thin pair of boxers.

I manage to angle my hips away as my cock lengthens. Prickles of heat run up my spine as the pain of the change comes right on me.

Fates, at best I'm going to scare the female to death if she feels my manhood moving against her ass. Especially because bear cock… it's huge. I'm not bragging, just stating fact. At worst, we could have a bear mauling situation.

No, I wouldn't hurt her. My bear would never hurt a woman.

Keep telling yourself that, a voice in the back of my head whispers. *You still don't know for sure.*

It's hotter than hell in the sleeping bag. I'm sweating like a demon, but I'm relieved to feel her flesh warm against mine. Her teeth stop chattering. The shivering ceases.

The poor female, probably exhausted from her ordeal, slips into a gentle slumber.

I whistle softly to her dog, who's pacing around us, keeping an eye on me, and I pat the spot on the other side of me. The loyal canine probably needs my body heat to warm up, too. He drops to his belly beside me, understanding. I scoot him against the sleeping bag, offering my side for him to mold into.

Now if I can just figure out how to stuff my bear back down and fall asleep with this king-sized boner.

CHAPTER 4

*M*iranda

THE FIRST THING I notice is the sound of gentle snoring.

Right beside my ear.

Then I realize how crazy-hot I am. Like sweaty-hot. And my slick skin is sliding over someone else's slick skin.

Oh God!

My eyes fly open as the memory of my rescue comes flooding back.

The beast of a man who threw me over his shoulder and brought me to his cabin is lying on his back beside me. My head rests on his arm, and—oh lordy, one of my legs is tossed over his, as if this is a post-coital snuggle rather than two perfect strangers lying naked in a sleeping bag together.

It's dim in the cabin, only the first rays of morning

light come through the windows, but a fire still burns in the hearth, illuminating the room with flickering amber light. I lift my head and stare at the stranger. He's enormous, his muscled chest and arms inked with black tattoos. He has high cheekbones with hollows beneath and sports an unruly dark beard, like some kind of mountain man.

I don't know if it's the wildness about him—the formidable appearance and the gruff manners, the remoteness of his cabin—but a spike of fear suddenly shoots through me.

What if this is the serial killer? Maybe he kidnaps women and brings them up to this very cabin.

I need to get out of this sleeping bag. And this cabin.

Stat.

Of course the zipper for the sleeping bag is on the other side.

I ease my leg off the giant of a man and start to slither my way straight up, out of the sleeping bag. And that's when I see the man's other arm.

His tattooed limb—the one not serving as a pillow for my head—is curved protectively around Bear.

My breath escapes in a relieved puff—almost a laugh.

The memory of him using a hairdryer on my best friend comes flooding back.

He can't be a serial killer. This man saved not only my life, but also Bear's.

He probably likes to keep the women alive so he can torture them, the whisper of fear tries to point out. *And serial killers can be dog lovers, too.*

The thing is, he's not a dog lover. I doubt he's much of a people lover either. He was grim and grudging in his help yesterday. Would a serial killer be grudging if he had me where he wanted me? No, he'd be celebrating.

That's what I tell myself, anyway.

None of that can be attributed to my newfound fascination with the man's burly chest. Or the way I'm suddenly even more intensely aware of my nudity. The slickness between my legs. My body's reacting to the sight of his sculpted muscles, the nearness of a naked male. *Is he naked?*

I peek inside the sleeping bag.

Boxer shorts.

And, um, morning wood.

Holy shit, his cock is huge!

My nipples tighten, a slow thrum begins between my legs.

I'm not sure when I've been this turned on. Of course it's been a long time since I've had sex. A really long time.

Three years long time and that was with Will Carter, another grad student who literally fucked me over, using me to help him sort through his research and dumping me as soon as he figured out what to do.

Which is why I don't do men. Or sex. Or relationships.

Observe the male of the species, poisoned by testosterone. Spurred by his competitive and antagonistic instincts, he views any intelligent woman as a threat...

Because being a woman in science has taught me one lesson very well: If I don't look out for myself and my research, I will never get anywhere. Sex, relationships, even friendships—they only screw your career in the end.

It doesn't help that the extra weight I carry makes me look like a fertility goddess instead of a serious science geek. And this man here got to see it all last night. Every pound of flesh on me.

My pussy clenches as if it suspects he liked what he saw, even though my brain tells me different.

It's crazy—not like me at all—but I slowly push the sleeping bag down to see more of the man's chest. I tell myself I just want to see the rest of the tattoos.

The ritual markings of the male, signals his pain tolerance and non-conformity to conservative ideals...

Hello, twelve-pack of abdominal muscles. His body is both lean and large at the same time. I'm tempted to touch the curls in his dark beard, but I know that would be going too far.

Bear lifts his head and thumps his tail.

I don't speak to my dog because I don't want to wake up my rescuer. Not until I crawl safely out of this sleeping bag and find some clothes. I continue my ridiculous shimmy, army crawling my way out of the bag and he snorts, curving up the arm that was under my head and is now at waist level and capturing me.

Oh crap.

My breast now brushes the top of his head, and my pussy's wetter than before just from feeling his strength.

I imagine him using that strength to hold me down and bring those sensuous lips to my nipple.

OMG, what? Okay, I'm crazy. Hold me down? Definitely not a fantasy I've ever had before. I don't go for cocky, dominant men who think they need to take charge in the relationship or bed.

Gross.

I try to keep shimmying, but his arm around my waist

bands tight, even though he's fallen back into gentle snores.

What kind of man tightens his grip on a woman when he sleeps?

A serial killer, the worrisome voice whispers.

I shake it off. No, that's not right. A man who is used to sleeping with a woman.

And I should find that sweet, but instead a knot of jealousy tightens in my belly. So this guy regularly brings women home to his cabin? Who are they? Women from town?

Okay, I give up. I'm going to have to risk waking the guy up. I'm starving and I have to pee. I clear my throat.

Nothing. He doesn't even stir.

I try to push the limb around my midsection away, but it doesn't budge. I clear my throat again.

"I, uh, need to get up," I finally say out loud.

He still doesn't stir.

Wow. Deep sleeper.

Well, screw polite. This guy has to let go. I push at the arm and struggle to get out of the sleeping bag, accidentally kneeing him in the ribs as I do.

He snorts and shakes his head, rolling over to his side and up to an elbow in a slow but fluid motion. He blinks like I just woke him from the dead. His eyes seem yellow at first, but it must be a reflection from the fire, because after he blinks, I realize they are very dark brown. Almost black.

Then his lids snap wide, because, yeah. He's got a curvy naked woman on her hands and knees beside his head. I'm sure he's getting more than an eyeful of way too many of my unclothed parts. After a quick debate between diving back under the sleeping bag covers and getting out, I choose getting out. Because I don't need to rub my bare body down the front of his bare body—*Stop, brain!*—I scramble out as fast as I can, covering my breasts with my forearm and my twat with my other hand.

The man makes an animal-sounding growl and his muscled arm swings through the air as he twists his body and reaches up behind him. The fire glints in his eyes again, giving them an animal-like glow.

A hunter green flannel shirt flies through the air at me, and I catch it with my face. I yank it on, buttoning quickly and pulling the hem down as far as it goes. He's a big guy, but I'm a big girl—curvy, I like to say because it feels better than overweight—and I fill the shirt so it barely drops below my crotch.

My face totally burns up as he watches me with dark eyes. I remember him carrying me out of the bathroom last night like I weighed nothing. Like I was the heroine in a movie.

I shake my head to dislodge that starry-eyed thought.

"Um, thanks," I mumble, backing up as he starts to crawl out of the sleeping bag.

He stops just before his hips emerge, and pulls the fabric up to his waist.

I can't help but look, because the reason he didn't come out is obvious.

Yep. Giant tent in the sleeping bag. Holy shit, that flag pole is high.

I turn away to give him some privacy.

Bathroom. That's what I need. I look around, not

remembering the layout from last night when I was too disoriented from the cold.

I must've had hypothermia.

A fresh rush of gratitude runs through me. Bear and I would both be dead if it wasn't for the man out there. Whose name I don't even know.

I find the bathroom and quickly pee. My clothes are still in a puddle on the floor where he discarded them yesterday. I remember those large hands disrobing me. It wasn't sexy—he'd been more disgruntled than anything—but the memory of it makes my nipples pucker again. I really wish I had a pair of panties to wear. Then the thrum between my legs wouldn't be so strong.

I pick my clothes up but they're wet and covered with dirt. Damn. I take a quick look in the mirror. Dear lord, I look like hell! My hair is a disaster from being in a hat all day yesterday and then rolling around on a beefy man's arm all night. I grab his comb and do my best to yank out the tangles. I open the bathroom cabinet.

I read a statistic once on bathroom cabinets. Something like fifty percent of people who use your bathroom will look in the cabinets. I don't normally fall into that group, but today's an exception. There's no mouthwash or extra toothbrush. There's very little, actually. Just the man-basics: deodorant, dental floss, and Vaseline which I grab and rub some on my dry, cracked lips.

I carry my bundle of wet clothes out.

Mountain man is up and he's put his jeans on, which somehow makes him look even hotter. The washboard abs look even finer when framed by denim. I lick up my lips—a nervous habit I thought I'd kicked years ago.

"Um, thanks. You know, for rescuing us. And um"—I look at the rumpled sleeping bag on the floor— "saving my life."

He has this strange way of remaining perfectly still. He watches me intently, his eyes so dark they appear black, his expression inscrutable.

And then he doesn't answer. Just turns and walks to the back door, opens it and whistles to Bear. Snow's still falling. My dog, who has somehow decided that this man is the boss, trots over and stops just short of going out, tail tucked.

"Out," Caleb grunts and nudges Bear. There's no anger in his voice, but it's impossibly firm and my dog instantly obeys, diving into a snow drift taller than him and disappearing.

I gasp because that means the snow appears to be over three feet deep.

Crap. I guess I'm not going anywhere. Not unless mountain man has snowshoes or skis I can borrow and he can point me in the right direction.

Bear does his business quickly and comes bounding back up the steps, snow coating his fur everywhere. He comes inside and shakes it all off onto the floor.

"Sorry," I say wryly.

Mountain man doesn't answer, just throws a towel down over the snow and walks away.

"Um, do you have a washing machine?" I try again.

He turns without answering.

I gasp when he snatches the clothes from my arms without a word and flips open the washer, which is right next to where we're standing by the back door. I didn't notice because the washer and dryer are cloaked by wooden cabinetry. He tosses my clothes in and starts it up.

When he turns, his gaze lands on my freshly-glossed lips.

I flush, imagining he's thinking about me going through his cabinets. His gaze travels down the length of my body, stopping at my bare legs. "You cold?" he rumbles. His voice is deep and just as gruff as I remembered it. It's also somehow pleasing. My body tingles in reaction. "I can get you some sweatpants."

I'm not cold, because the cabin is toasty with the fire, but I definitely want pants. I lick my lips again—*dammit, I have to break that habit!*—and bob my head. "I—yes. That would be nice, thank you."

He walks away without a response. If I weren't so uncomfortable at waking up spooning this man *naked*, I might appreciate his economy of words. As it is, I would give anything for some kind of normal conversation. Some chit chat to put me at ease, like, "My name is Joe Mountain, you had quite a scare yesterday, didn't you? How are you feeling now? Can I make you some breakfast?"

Actually, as I imagine that scenario, it sounds too much like what a serial killer might say. As long as this guy remains surly, it probably means he's not interested in cutting me into pieces and burying me in the basement.

Right?

∼

Caleb

. . .

MY BRAIN KEEPS STUTTERING over the fuck-hot body on that female in my living room.

Knowing her pussy is bare right now does something visceral to me. My bear came out of slumber hella fast the moment I woke up face to thigh with her. It's a wonder I didn't shift right there.

And her scent: arousal.

I can't imagine why she was turned on. I thought she'd be terrified to come to her senses and find herself naked in a sleeping bag with a stranger. And I think she was. But she was also turned on.

I never thought a human female could smell so good. I certainly didn't expect to be so affected by another female's scent. Bears don't normally mate for life, but this one did.

So I'm unnerved by my body—and my bear's—reaction to her. It feels like a betrayal of Jen's memory.

So I stay in my bedroom far longer than it takes to grab a pair of sweatpants and try not to wonder how she'll look in them. I take my time, put on a t-shirt, pace around my room a few times.

Damn the voluptuous female for interfering with my solitude!

When I emerge, I toss the pants in her direction, trying not to look at the way her braless breasts stretch the fabric of my flannel. The way the taut points of her nipples protrude. I'm suddenly rocked by a vision of me making those full breasts bounce in a variety of ways that all involve me pounding into her from different angles. My bear rumbles against the cage of humanity.

Stop!

What the fuck is wrong with me?

I pad to the kitchenette to find us some food. I'm hangry as hell, and I'll bet she is too. Food will calm the bear down.

"What's your name?" Her voice starts off wobbly but finishes on a strong note, like she's forcing herself to be assertive.

"Caleb." I don't dare look at her. Not when all I can think about is making those breasts dance. I open the refrigerator and pull out two packages of bacon, the eggs, milk and butter.

"I'm Miranda." Her voice is musical to my ears. Her name is a goddamn song. I can't stop myself from taking a look.

Fuck, she's beautiful. Her auburn hair tumbles in tangled waves across her shoulders. Her eyes are green, with lashes I can barely see because they're the same color as her hair. The uneasy expression on her face makes me turn quickly away.

I fire up the two front gas burners and put frying pans on them to heat, then pull out a bowl and the box of pancake mix. "Just Miranda? Not Doctor Somebody?" Fates, am I making chit chat?

That's not like me at all. I don't talk much. To anyone. I especially don't make useless conversation to make people feel more comfortable.

Apparently now I do.

She lets out a surprised laugh—a sound that instantly relaxes my bear. "Well, I do have a doctorate. But no one calls me that." Her voice turns suspicious. "What made you think I'm a Ph.D.?"

"Research lab," I grunt. "I saw you driving up there yesterday."

Not a lie.

I leave out the part where I rubbed my nose on her window looking in at her prancing around in her little tank top.

I arrange one package of bacon in the frying pan and then crack six eggs into a bowl to make a large batch of pancakes.

"Why don't you use the title? I imagine you worked hard for those letters." I risk another glance over my shoulder at her.

Damn. She's no less enticing in my sweatpants. She fills them out with her ample hips and curvy ass. They're too long for her, of course, but she's pulled them up and rolled the waistband down until it rests on her hip bones. Fuck, she's beautiful.

Surprise flits over her face at my words. I don't even know what made me say them, just that I have a feeling she doesn't demand enough respect from the people around her.

"I don't like to be pretentious," she says, but her brows drop down. "Although I guess all the men in my department insist they be called *Doctor*."

"What department is that?"

Mark it down. This must be a record for the most conversation I've made in three years.

The bacon starts to sizzle as I combine the ingredients for the pancakes and pull a package of frozen wild blueberries out of the freezer.

"Ecology. That's a lot of packages of blueberries in

your freezer." Her voice is close, like she walked into the kitchen. Well, it's technically all one room—kitchen, dining, living room. One main area, two bedrooms and a bath. I built it myself for my mate.

She opens my freezer. I bristle at having her in my kitchen, in the space Jen used to occupy, but then I have another problem.

"Wow. So trout and blueberries. Do you eat anything else?"

I cringe inwardly. My freezer is packed with bear food. It probably looks strange to a human.

"I eat bacon," I grunt, flipping the pancakes. "And pancakes." Then, to distract her, I say, "How are you feeling today? Any numbness or pain in your fingers or toes? Ears? Tip of your nose?" I didn't see anything that looked like frostbite last night, but I also was in a hurry to get her in the sleeping bag and warmed up, so it's not like I gave her a thorough examination.

And that thought shouldn't give me a throbbing hard on, but it does.

My nostrils flare and I swivel my hips more firmly away from her so she won't see her effect on me.

"Um, no. I think I'm okay. Thanks to you."

Her hesitant gratitude creates a surprising warmth in my chest. Which is dumb. I certainly didn't expect or desire her thanks.

"I'm not even going to ask what the hell you were doing out there, because I'm pretty sure it's gonna make me want to turn you over my knee."

She draws in a sharp breath.

Oh fuck. I shouldn't have said that.

I give her my back, turning the bacon, piling pancakes onto a plate and tossing one down to her dog. Over the scent of the bacon and pancakes, I catch her scent.

That sweet arousal.

Fuck me now.

Seriously? She's turned on by my comment? I didn't need to know that.

I really didn't.

Because now I can't stop thinking about just how much I'd love to bend her over and smack that ass red for nearly freezing to death.

"That was entirely inappropriate." Her voice sounds strangled.

I'm not asshole enough not to turn around now. I find her cheeks flushed pink, eyes snapping. The way her chest rises and falls too quickly makes me think of how I'd like to make her lose her breath in other ways.

"You're right," I admit. "I'm a dick. And I don't get company too often. I'm rusty on what to say to a woman I stripped naked but didn't fuck."

Oh for fates' sake! Now I'm really digging a hole.

The scent of her arousal grows stronger. "Okay, probably you'd better stop before it gets worse," she warns and I'm surprised to feel my lips quirk at the edges.

My cock lengthens down the leg of my jeans.

"Who are you?" she demands suddenly, like she senses my differences. That I'm an entirely different species from her.

I turn back to the stove, pouring three neat circles of batter on the frying pan and dropping frozen blueberries onto them. "I'm no one."

Of course that sounds entirely suspicious. The scent of her arousal disappears, replaced the metallic scent of fear.

She's probably been warned about that missing women up here. Does she think I'm the killer?

I rack my brain to think of something to say that will put her at ease, but nothing occurs to me. All I can think to do is to make breakfast and keep my mouth shut. I put a coffee pot on to brew, then scoop the first package of bacon out of the frying pan and put in another. "Here," I grunt, dropping the plate piled high with pancakes and a plate with bacon onto the small table that sits by the window. The window which is halfway covered by a snowdrift. Her dog follows closely, pleading eyes on me.

"You must be hungry." I slide the plate of butter onto the table, along with the jug of honey.

She stands over the table while I pour some coffee, her nervous energy making me want to go back into hibernation. It's my default response to anything that requires emotion. Or effort. Or any spark of living.

I hand her a plate and fork and lift my chin to the chair at the table. She takes them wordlessly and sits down. I toss a piece of bacon to the dog, sit down across from her and slather my pile of pancakes with honey.

She watches me dubiously. "Sweet tooth, eh?"

I look down at the amount of honey on the cakes as I take a huge bite. I suppose it is a lot. I shrug. "I guess," I say with my mouth full. "I like honey."

I think I detect amusement in her expression, but we eat without speaking. I shouldn't care whether she likes the food or not, but my bear is stupidly pleased when she cleans her plate and reaches for seconds.

"Well, what now? I don't suppose you have a snowmobile here? Or some other way for me to get back to the research cabin?"

I get up and retrieve the second batch of bacon and set it on the table. "Doctor M, you're not going anywhere."

CHAPTER 5

*M*iranda

TWO THOUGHT wheels turn at once. One—he called me *doctor,* which shows respect, even admiration. Except two —he just implied I have no choice in the matter of whether I'm leaving or not.

It's the second thought I get hitched up on. "Excuse me?" The feminist in me rears her head, ready to defend myself against yet another man who thinks he can control me.

Caleb—the surly mountain man with twelve-pack abs arches a brow right back at me. "You heard me." He takes a bite of bacon. By *bite* I mean he crunches off half of three slices at once and chews them slowly while giving me the stink eye.

I try to interpret his words. I mean, I suppose it's obvious I can't leave. That's probably what he's saying.

But I don't like the way he said it. Because he's either being a controlling asshole or he's the psychopathic killer who plans to keep me here and bury me in the basement.

Okay, I don't think the cabin actually has a basement, but in the backyard, then.

"You're saying I can't leave?"

"Yep. That's what I'm saying."

I narrow my eyes. "Are you going try and stop me?"

"Sure am. You know why? Cause even if you can hike more than ten feet from this cabin in drifts that are already up to your chest—which I seriously doubt you can—the trail's covered and you don't know your way back. You'll likely fall into a drift and this time end up with frostbite. Then I'll have to go out in the cold and drag you back." He finishes his epic speech by taking a gulp of coffee.

I fold my arms across my chest. He isn't wrong. I just don't want to be stuck in a remote cabin with Mr. Grumpy for days. Even if Mr. Grumpy also happens to be Mr. Tall, Dark, Tattooed and Bearded with a sexy mountain man vibe. *Especially* because of that.

"Fine. I'm not going anywhere. But for the record, I didn't choose to be stuck up here with you."

"Makes two of us." He glowers at me behind his coffee mug. "What the hell made you come all the way up here in this weather anyway?"

"I didn't think it was going to be this bad," I say through a clenched jaw. "And it wasn't snowing when I left the research cabin yesterday. The storm came up suddenly, and I got disoriented. I'm not stupid." I get up and take our dishes to the sink.

"Didn't think you were, Doctor M." He emphasizes

doctor. Is he mocking me?

"I am under a deadline. I need this data., it's important." There's no dishwasher, so I start washing the dishes
by hand and put them in the drying rack.

"Not worth your life," he mutters. I steal a look over
my shoulder. Something in his expression reminds me of
Dr. Alogore and my smirking colleagues.

"You know what? Forget it. You wouldn't understand."

"What's that supposed to mean?" His black eyes flash
with a glint of yellow. Great, I've antagonized him. Probably not the best idea, but riling him up gives me a shot of
satisfaction. I get the feeling he hasn't talked to, much less
verbally sparred with anyone in awhile. Well, he said as
much already, didn't he? "I'm not stupid either,
sweetheart."

"Please do not call me *sweetheart.*" I point a finger
at him.

He shrugs. "You're in my cabin. You'll have to put up
with my ways. I mean no harm by it."

I snort. "It's patronizing."

"Lady, what's your problem?"

The *lady* gets to me, too. "You wanna know?" I throw
my hands up. "You want to know what my problem is? My
problem is every man I've ever met tries to tell me what to
do. Treats me like a doormat and tramples all over me. I
have news for you, buddy." My voice rises now. "You
think you're God's gift to the green earth, and women are
just here to massage your egos, suck your cocks and, I
don't know, be eye candy. But we're not. We're not here
for you."

Caleb stares at me like I'm a hissing goose. Which I

guess I am. It's weird but it feels good to give a man a piece of my mind for a change. Something I can't ever do back at the lab, since the entire science world is ruled by men. One wrong word and you're forever passed over for the good positions.

"I don't know what a man did to you, but there's no reason to take it out on me."

Finished with the dishes, I slump into a chair. "You're right. I'm sorry. I'm just frustrated to be stranded here without my computer. I have so much to do and no way to do it." Bear comes and licks my hand.

"And I'd rather be asleep on the couch. But we're stuck together, so we might as well make the best of it."

The washing machine buzzes and I surge to my feet, grateful for something—anything to do. I throw my clothes in the dryer and start it up.

Everything in the cabin is neat and clean. Well-maintained. It's simple and rustic, but not completely without creature comforts. For example, I noticed there was a garbage disposal in the kitchen sink. And there are ceiling fans in the living area.

Observe the rustic mountain man in his natural habitat...

I clear my throat. "Do you suppose it will snow all day?"

Caleb looks out the window. "Might. Either way, you won't be leaving. I'd count on staying at least one more night here. Maybe two if it doesn't stop snowing." He lifts his chin in the direction of what must be the bedrooms. "You can take the room on the left. There's sheets in the top drawer of the dresser."

"Thank you." I'm regretting my outburst. It's strange I felt comfortable enough to get snappish with a stranger. Maybe the manner we spent the night last night has something to do with it. "I do appreciate your hospitality. I didn't mean to sound—"

He waves me off. "Save it. I don't require an apology. Not when my manners are shit."

Well. That shouldn't make my chest turn all warm and fluttery. I have no idea why I'm so attracted to this man.

I head into the bedroom to put the sheets on the bed. It's painted in lavender. A single twin bed stands against one wall, the mattress bare. I find sheets in the drawer, like he said. Flowered sheets.

Caleb definitely doesn't strike me as the purple-walled flowered sheets kind of man. Not even for a guest bed. So who bought the sheets? Did they come with the place? Maybe he rents and his landlord provided them. Except I feel certain it's his place. It just reflects him so well.

I make the bed and throw the folded comforter I find in the closet—also flowered in bright cheery colors—over the top. I should just stay in this room and give him some space. The place is small and he didn't ask for a guest, after all.

Except it's chillier in the room. There's no fire. And nothing to do.

Oh, who am I kidding? There's no Caleb. And I'm drawn to the man like a bear to honey.

I head back into the main area, suddenly remembering I should have my iPad and tree ring samples in my backpack. That would give me something to work on.

"Caleb?"

He jerks and I smother a laugh. The man fell asleep in the few minutes I was out of the room. I guess he didn't sleep well last night with me plastered up against his body.

"Did I have a backpack on when you rescued me?"

"Erm, yes." He rubs his face and surges to his feet. His long legs flex powerfully and he makes the movement look graceful despite his large size and the low couch. He retrieves my backpack from behind the front door. "Here you go."

"Thank God," I breathe, more to myself than to him. "I can start cataloguing."

~

Caleb

DAMN, this female is going to drive me apeshit. And not just because she's a pain in the ass—which she is. More because being trapped in this small space with her is doing raunchy things to my bear.

Ideally I could just go to my bedroom, shut the door and sleep until it's time for her to leave. But humans don't hibernate, and she would think it's weird. Plus, she keeps waking me up for shit.

She bustles past me, muttering to herself, "The male of the species masters only the most basic life skills. More advanced nesting techniques are left to the female, who will create a nurturing environment for her offspring—"

"What the fuck?" I blurt and she whirls, face red.

"What?" Her lips move, shaping excuses. "Um, did I

say that out loud? Sorry, I entertain myself by pretend narrating. It's just a stupid game."

Damn, her face is so cute. With her flushed cheeks and parted lips, she looks freshly fucked and pleasured.

No. No. No. Do not think about that…

"Just—" I wave my hand towards the opposite end of the cabin. "Stay over there."

Great. Way to be hospitable.

She stomps off, muttering something about, "Long periods of isolation can result in loss of basic courtesy and knowledge of social interactions…"

I'm thankful when she falls silent, but nothing helps me forget she's there. Having her here is a special form of torture. I can't just hang around doing nothing with her all up in my space. Her strawberries and vanilla ice cream scent tickles my nose. Her uppity feminist sensibilities riles my temper. Her curvy body looks so ripe for a pounding. My bear claws to the surface so fast my vision changes. I blink rapidly, shoving him back down.

Shit! Stop thinking about pounding her.

Stop. Thinking.

Maybe what I should do is go into the bedroom and jack off. Just to take the pressure off. My cock twitches against my jeans in favor of that idea.

But the cabin's so quiet she'd probably hear me.

Christ, why don't I have a television? Radio? Anything to create some comfortable distance between me and this human female?

CHAPTER 6

*M*iranda

CALEB SNOOZES behind a *National Geographic* with grizzly bears on the cover most of the morning. He doesn't move from the couch until lunchtime, when he makes us turkey sandwiches, which he serves with a bowl of mixed nuts.

I help clean up the kitchen, then sit down and catalogue the few tree ring samples I took. When I finish, I take notes on my tablet for my research, then spend a few hours editing a proposal I happened to save onto the tablet as well. There's no WiFi and my cell phone doesn't work, so I can't check emails or get any business correspondence done.

When I've exhausted all the work I can do without my laptop, I turn off the tablet.

"Well, I'm out of things to do," I announce, even

though Caleb's not into conversation. "I can't believe you don't have any games. A pack of cards. A puzzle. Something. Anything."

I go to the window and press my face against the glass. Despite nearly freezing to death yesterday, I find the snow beautiful.

"Trivial Pursuit?" I ask hopefully, even though I already know the answer. "It's my favorite." I'm babbling but the silence is getting to me. "My last boyfriend hated playing it with me because I always won. Have you ever played?"

"No."

"My ex said it was a waste of time, learning all those useless facts, but I think he was just a sore loser." I spin away from the window and go back to pacing the floor. His cabin is curiously devoid of almost anything personal, although it's quite comfortable. There are throw rugs on the floor and the walls are painted pretty colors—apple green and cheery yellow. The decor doesn't really seem like grumpy mountain man.

Except in other ways it seems very much like him. Custom cabinets that might have been hand-hewn and carved. A gorgeous slab of polished burl wood made into a coffee table. Did he make them? He seems like a man who works with his hands.

I eye them. Very large, calloused hands.

I shiver, remembering those hands stripped me bare, helped me gently into a tub of tepid water last night. What would it feel like to be caressed by those hands?

Or even... held down. Manhandled. Fucked roughly.

Yeah, not by the hands, but by the man. Wow. I can't believe I'm having these thoughts.

The mating habits of the human species. The male preens and flexes his muscles. He feeds and cares for the female, proving he will be a suitable mate with the ability to provide for their young. The female pretends not to notice, but it's only a matter of time before she finds an excuse to brush against his big, burgeoning cock. The resulting mating dance involves fornication on the couch, on the floor, on the kitchen table...

Ack! My mock-u-mentory is turning into porn. "Cabin Sex Fever: Innocent researcher rescued by mountain man shows her gratitude." I'd totally get off to that. Especially if Caleb was in a starring role.

I scrub a hand across my heated face. Maybe freezing and nearly dying in the woods boosts your hormone levels to epic proportions.

Caleb glowers at me from his chair. Bear watches me without moving from his slumped position on the floor near Caleb's feet. It's weird how my dog seems to think Caleb is his master now. I guess he's a sexist pig, too, deferring to the man in the room. Traitor.

"Come on." I clap my hands. "Let's play a game."

"No."

"Truth or dare?"

"Pass."

"Please," I plead. "What else are we going to do?"

Caleb mutters something that sounds suspiciously like, "Thought a brainiac scientist would be quieter."

I wrinkle my nose at him. "We can either play something or I can tell you more about my research."

"No."

"My current project is about the effect of climate change on the tree population in New Mexico. I'm using samples from ponderosa pine trees to look at what's happened over the last one hundred years or more."

Caleb grunts.

I know he's not really interested, but since he goaded me with that quieter comment, I can't help but give it back to him. I settle in to explain the details of my grant-funded research. "Basically, I've plotted an area near the research cabin and now I have to take a sample from every tree within the plot. I started last fall, but the plot didn't prove big enough, so I'm back up here to gather a larger sample size."

Caleb's sensuous lips tighten, but he doesn't look away. He's staring me down with an unnerving animal-like intensity.

I plow on anyway. "My preliminary research shows a significant effect on the trees. When I put this together with my research from whitebark pine, I should have a real case to make. Especially with the whitebark pine. It's a keystone species in Colorado and Wyoming. Its decline has a direct affect on wildlife, especially the brown bears, who rely on its pine nuts to eat."

For some reason, Caleb seems to find that interesting. He cocks his head and opens his mouth like he's going to say something, but then his beard shakes along with his head like he changed his mind. "So what'd these men do to you?"

"What? What men?" I look around the room as if to see the imaginary men.

"The ones you mentioned before. The ones who treat you like a doormat." He frowns when he says it, and his fists clench. If Dr. Alogore or one of the Dockers-wearing brigade were here, they would look pale and flabby beside Caleb's physical perfection. I take perverse pleasure in this.

"Never mind," I wave a hand. "They're not important. I was wrong, anyway, to lump you in with them."

"Did they hurt you?"

"What?" My eyes widen at the tension rippling up his muscled arms. It's breathtaking, really. I've never met a man like him before. So rugged and coarse, but not unkind. And clearly bothered by any injustice that may have been done to me.

Wow.

"No. Not at all. Well, unless you count emotional and career distress. They're just... chauvinists. And not respectful. They treat me like a pretty piece of ass. Or their personal research assistant. Or worse—a secretary."

His nostrils flare. "Do they touch you without your consent?" he growls. The hair on the back of my neck stands up, but my nipples also harden. Something about this rugged mountain man saying the word *consent*. Oooh, sexy. Shiver.

"No, nothing like that." I toss my hair back. "It's just that they don't respect my contributions. My brain is only useful in a support role for their projects. They don't value my research. They never invite me to take the lead on anything, only to do all the hard work—writing the proposals and research papers—and then they put their names on the publications above mine."

Caleb mutters something.

"What was that?" I cock a hand to my ear, ready to chew him out for some sexist comment.

He clears his throat. "Then they're idiots." He looks me straight in the eye.

I swallow.

"Any guy would be lucky to have you on their team. You're clearly a hard-working, driven scientist who knows her shit."

Well, how nice. "Thank you—"

"But it would be hard for them to ignore that you're easy on the eyes."

Swing and miss. I roll my eyes at him. "Truth or dare."

He shakes his head.

"I just did mine. It was truth. It's your turn."

He groans.

"Truth it is. Why are you up here all alone?"

"None of your business," he growls and picks up his chair, turning it to face the fireplace and dropping it with a thud. Bear gives a little whine.

"Fine then." I go back to pacing.

Boredom stretches. I can't stand not being busy—not working, especially in the middle of the afternoon. I usually work until I can't think anymore and then I let myself be brain dead and watch *The Bachelor* or *The Voice*. I actually have a few episodes of *The Bachelor* saved on my tablet, but if I'm going to be here all day, maybe more, I figure I should save them for later. Tonight, when I'm ready for bed and need to wind down.

Caleb doesn't even have a television. And he doesn't seem to mind doing nothing.

I seriously don't get it.

"What do you do for work?" I ask him. "When you're not snowed in?"

"Construction. Road crew. Pick up work."

I raise a brow. "In the winter?"

One corner of his mouth quirks in a crooked smile. "Smart woman. Nah, not in the winter. I usually rest up in the winter. But last month I did a little cage fighting for money."

My eyes fly wide, the image of him, naked to the waist, fists cocked flashing far too easily into my mind. I hate boxing—never watch any form of fights—but for some reason I'm turned on. All my lady parts activate, my nipples getting hard, clit buzzing.

The dominance display of a male in his prime never fails to attract the females of the species, no matter how refined...

Seriously. Must be the aftereffects of hypothermia. I'm never this much of a horn dog. Especially over a He-man like Caleb.

"I'll bet you kick some serious ass," I muse, more to myself than to him.

He raises his brows, like he's surprised, then shrugs. "Last match was a forfeit, which was a huge fucking disappointment for me, even though I took home the winnings. I didn't even get to fight."

I drag my lower lip through my teeth. I swear I feel his testosterone washing over my body like a warm wave.

What made me think I hated men?

This one makes all those qualities I usually hate seem admirable.

To distract myself from undressing him in my mind, I get up and search the kitchen, making myself at home. "You know what I'm craving?"

Caleb grunts.

"Hot chocolate. Do you have hot chocolate?" I rummage through cupboards.

"What do you think?" Caleb sounds disgusted.

"It doesn't need to be the mix. I can use any chocolate bar... melt it down or something." I grab an unmarked bottle. "What's this?"

"Nothing."

I shake the bottle and it sloshes. "Doesn't sound like nothing." I pop the cork and take a whiff. Pure grain alcohol sears my nose and I sputter. "Whew, hello." I cough. "What is this, one thousand proof?"

"No." Caleb's at my side, reaching for the bottle. I didn't even see him move. "Put it back. That stuff is stronger than you can imagine."

"No." I hide the bottle behind my back, pleased I've gotten him out of his chair. He crowds me against the cabinets. "It's mine now."

"I'm warning you. It's way too strong for a hum—I mean woman."

"Were you going to say *human*?" I laugh. "Finders keepers."

"What you gonna do, drink it?" He crosses his arms in front of his chest, making his biceps bulge beautifully.

"Maybe I will." I pull the bottle out from behind my back and eye it. It's a little intimidating in its brown bottle. I sniff the rim. Smells a bit like turpentine. Maybe it's not really drinkable.

Caleb towers over me. He's all in my space and my body seems to love it. I touch my tongue to the glass.

"You wouldn't," he says.

Now I have something to prove. "Bottoms up." I take a swig.

Next thing I know I'm bent over, gasping, as lighter fluid sears my insides.

"Miranda," he yelps, and pounds my back. There's a smoking pit where my stomach used to be. It's the first time he's said my name, and I like the way it sounds. Especially with that note of concern.

"Damn," I cough, my eyes streaming. "That really cleans out the pipes."

"I thought you were going to take a sip, not drink half the damn bottle." He must have saved the bottle from tumbling out of my nerveless hands, because he sets it on the counter with a thud.

"Your turn," I rasp.

"No way." He propels my willing body into a chair.

"You're the one who wanted it back. I dare you."

"No."

I point to the bottle. "Chicken."

His eyes narrow. Inwardly, I crow. I don't know what possesses me to harass this guy, but now that I'm sure he's actually a gentleman, I love goading him. *The female tests the male to make sure he's worthy in a form of flirtation...*

Growling under his breath, he stalks to the counter, grips the bottle's neck and takes a pull. I eye him, waiting for signs of distress. Nothing. *Nada.* Not a cough or an eye twitch. Caleb is badass.

Meanwhile, the alcohol isn't so much hitting my

bloodstream as blazing a fiery trail through each and every limb. I pump my fist in the air and I whoop. "Truth or dare!"

Caleb sits across from me, his fist clenched on the bottle. "Oh, no. It's your turn."

"All right." I lick my lips. His gaze snaps to my mouth. Dammit, I gotta stop. "Um... truth." I don't think I can take a dare quite yet, especially if it involves turpentine flavored moonshine.

"Where's your man?"

"What?" My mouth moves slowly now. In fact, my whole face is a bit numb. I pat my lips until I realize what I'm doing. "What man are you talking about?"

"The man whose ass I'm gonna kick for letting you come up here alone and unescorted."

My brow wrinkles as I try to figure out who he's talking about. "Man whose ass you're gonna kick... you mean my boss?"

"No, but I don't like him either." His growl shakes the table. Dr. Alogore is definitely on his shit list. Scary mountain man is intimidating. I definitely wouldn't want to be on his bad side. I mean, in a non-flirty way. Oh God—am I flirting?

I never flirt!

"I mean your man. Don't tell me a woman like you doesn't have a man." By the way he sweeps my body with his gaze, things suddenly become crystal clear.

"Whoa, whoa, whoa." I wave my hands. Damn, is it hot in here? I unbutton a couple buttons on the flannel shirt. "Um." I refocus on Caleb. "Those are a lot of assumptions for you to be making, buddy. First of all, I do not have a man. It is not a requirement for a woman like me or anyone to be attached to someone with a penis. I am not 'had'… by anyone. Ever."

His eyes darken. "Are you saying you're a virgin?"

"What?" I snort. Very unladylike snort. His shirt flops open on me and I twitch it back. "No. I def… definitely…" I speak slowly and enunciate, "have had sex. I just don't have a boyfriend. They are a waste of time and brain cells. They want someone to stick their dicks into and make them feel good about themselves, and they don't give anything in return. Men just take. I don't have the energy for that. I've got important work to do. Trees to… sample."

Caleb grunts. He takes another pull of the bottle. My eyes fix on the hooch. I wave a hand. "Give that here."

He doesn't relinquish it, but he holds it to my mouth and lets some dribble in.

"Hey!" I wipe my mouth, savoring the numbness on my tongue. "That's not enough."

"I think you've had plenty, sweetheart."

"Don't call me that." I shudder. "Dr. Alogore calls me that. Makes me want to puke."

"Maybe you should get your man to talk to him." Caleb looks like he wants to stab something.

"Don't have a man. Imma own womma." I smack my lips, trying to get feeling in them, and try again. "My. Own. Woman. I can take care o' myself."

"Hmm," Caleb says against the rim of the bottle.

"Whadda ya mean, hmmm. You said that very…" I give him side eye.

"I mean, you need a man."

"Please." I slap the table with my hand. "I don't need a man or anyone."

"I mean… you should have a man. Woman like you."

I raise a brow.

"Beautiful," he says and the world turns pink. *La vie en rose.* I thought it was only a song. *Arousal mimics intoxication, and vice versa. Combining the two can be dangerous…*

"Thank you."

"You need to eat more," Caleb says accusingly. He pushes away from the table, rummages in the cabinet. Comes back with a bar of chocolate.

"O-M-Gee." I grab it with both hands. "I love you." The numbness has moved elsewhere, probably to terrorize my liver. Food is just what I need.

He drops in his seat across from me, looking pleased. He doesn't even blink when I rip off the wrapper and cram the chocolate in my mouth with both hands. I eat like a chipmunk preparing for winter, and look up at him with both cheeks full.

"You would make someone a lovely boyfriend."

"No," he mutters, and I agree happily.

"No, you're right. You're a grouch. But saving my life, making me breakfast, giving me chocolate…" I give him a thumbs up. "Did I thank you, by the way?"

"Yeah."

I wipe my mouth and say it again. "Thank you for saving my life."

"No problem."

"And for calling me beautiful."

His gaze shoots up and meets mine and I'm stunned. A

ripple goes through my body—a shockwave of desire. The room, the snow outside: everything is the same. And everything is different.

"Um, that was nice of you," I whisper.

"No problem," he says to the tabletop.

I finish my chocolate. "Sorry, I should've saved some for you."

"It's okay." He has a strange look on his face. "You can make it up to me. Your turn. Truth."

"Me?" Is it my turn? "Wait, that's not how it works. I get to choose."

"Truth," he insists. "Why don't you have a man?"

"You mean a boyfriend?"

"I mean a man," he emphasizes firmly.

"Why don't you?" I retort. He shakes his head. I sigh. I do owe him for the candy bar. "Truth? I don't like sex."

"What?" He freezes.

"I said I don't like sex." I lift my chin. "It's completely overrated."

"Overrated."

"Yeah, you know," I wave my hand. In for a penny, in for a pound. "All this wooing and all the love songs, and what they write in romance novels. It's not true. Sex is messy, sometimes it's downright gross. At least it lasts only a few minutes."

"A few minutes," Caleb repeats disbelievingly.

"Yeah." I get defensive. "Don't tell me you take longer or something. Every guy thinks he's God's gift to women and... well, it's just disappointing."

I fiddle with the candy wrapper. The heat of Caleb's...

emotion or something emanates from him. Sears me across the distance between us.

Caleb sets the bottle down with a decisive thump. I jump as his chair scrapes backwards and he prowls around the table, plants a hand in front of me and on the back of my chair, and leans in close.

"Are you telling me"—his eyes rove up and down my face—"that a woman who looks like you, with that hot as fuck body… has never known pleasure by a man?"

Caleb the mountain man, pulling no punches.

My pussy clenches. Heat feathers across my skin.

"Um—"

He lays a big hand on my collarbone, his thumb finding my pulse and lightly stroking. Holy hell, my body comes alive. The angel choir is singing, and he's barely even touching me.

"Body like this was made to be stripped naked. Stroked all over." His voice seeps into secret places. I usually hate —despise—being reduced to a pair of big tits. Objectification of women makes me crazy. But my body responds to his every word. His eyes meet mine with the impact of a stun gun. The light hits them at a strange angle, making them appear yellow instead of brown. "…worshipped. I would take so much time…" His hand cups the back of my neck, massaging. I melt. Ten seconds, and I'm butter on a hot griddle. "Countless orgasms," he murmurs. "Endless pleasure. The fact that you haven't met a man to give you all that, baby… it's a crime against humanity."

I open my mouth but can't make a sound.

"First thing I'd do, Dr. M"—he stares at my lips—"is

take that mouth. That pouty, smart mouth. I'd kiss you until you couldn't keep still. Then I'd pin your arms above your head, hold you down and kiss you some more." He inhales deeply, like he can't get enough of my scent. His eyes rove over me as potent as any touch. Tingles start at my breasts and spread outward. "Then I'd undress you, slowly. Kiss you some more. Find out where to touch. What makes you sigh. I'd taste you"—he swallows, and I gulp in some air— "all over. Everywhere." His voice deepens. Ripples spread through my body, pulling me under. "And then…"

A long pause.

"And then?" I squeak.

He blows out a breath. I lean in close and he goes tense.

"No," he says.

"No?"

"This is a bad idea." He retreats.

My mouth falls open.

"We shouldn't. I shouldn't…" He rubs his hand over his face. "Forget what I said."

"What?" I'm on my feet. "You can't just… say all those things to me and then back off!"

"Miranda—" Confusion flits over his face.

"Countless orgasms? Endless pleasure?" I wave my arms. "Taste me all over? You can't say those things to a… a… sexually deprived woman and then just leave me hanging."

He stares at me, pain around his eyes, mirroring my own.

I take a deep breath and say the most outrageous thing

I've ever said, much less thought. "You have to show me what you got."

"No."

"Caleb! Please?" I gesture to the bedroom.

He narrows his eyes at me. "It's a bad idea."

I rise, sending my chair flying. Ignoring the crash behind me, I slam my hand on the table. "You know what I think? You're all talk and no walk."

"Excuse me?" he growls.

"That's right. You heard me. You're scared I'll find you lacking."

"I am not scared." He comes at me again, big muscle man. I have his number.

"You are too." I puff out my chest and my nipples poke him. My knees wobble but I hold my ground. "You're up here, hiding from the world, a big fat chicken."

"Miranda—"

"Bwook bwook bwook," I do my best chicken imitation. It is a fabulous imitation—very authentic.

"Miranda—"

"Bwaka! Bwaka!" I chicken dance in front of him. Not the sexiest way to signal my arousal, but judging by the way his jeans tent and a red flush creeps up his neck, it's working. I flap my arms and bob my head. *The mating call of the ecologist PhD. The female approaches the rugged male and shakes her plumage.* He is stunned.

A glance down makes me realize his flannel shirt has flapped open again, and I am flashing Caleb over and over.

"Oops." I go to rebutton when a hand grips my wrist.

"Don't bother." He's breathing hard.

"What?" I start, and he twists my arm behind my back,

bringing me flush against his body. His rock hard, very aroused body.

"You asked for it," he rasps a second before he drops his head and claims my mouth.

Caleb

I CAN'T STOP MYSELF. The curvy scientist has a long hard fuck coming and someone's got to give it to her. She needs to know that not all men are takers. That sex should feel good. That she's got a body built for pleasure.

The scent of her arousal intoxicates me more than my hooch intoxicated her. I slant my lips over her mouth, taking it. Owning it. My tongue sweeps between her lips, I taste the alcohol and chocolate on her breath.

Stop. Back off.

She's drunk.

You're taking advantage.

Reason attempts to seep in, but my bear's not having it. He claws to the surface and my teeth lengthen.

Christ, bear. Really? A mating bite? My bear is fucking insane.

I force myself to break the kiss and step back. "Doctor, you've had too much to drink to make good decisions."

She twists the fabric of my shirt in her fists and pulls my lips down to hers again. I give in for a moment, tasting her, devouring her.

And the teeth lengthen again.

Fuck. I have no control. I yank back. And then because I don't have the skills to verbally spar with her, I throw her over my shoulder and carry her to the guest room.

Gretchen's room. That quiets my bear.

I ease her down on the bed and back up to the doorway, to remove the urge to climb right on top of her. "Have a little nap, Doctor. Sleep it off. Come see me when you're sober if you still want a lesson in what a real man can do." I'm taunting her like a jackass, maybe half-hoping she'll be so turned off by my arrogance she'll keep her distance.

My cock strains at my jeans, not down with this plan of leaving her on the bed. Alone.

She stares up at me with green eyes. Innocence mingled with intelligence. Drunkenness with desire.

I take another step back. I need to get somewhere I can breathe. Somewhere I can stuff my bear back down.

"You're a patronizing ass."

I grin because I like when she gives it back to me. I like her resistance, her sass. "Not patronizing, just an ass. And you're tipsy. Sleep it off."

I shut the door firmly, like she's an errant child I sent to bed. Maybe I am patronizing. I give my cock a brutal squeeze through my jeans and grind my teeth.

This female will be the death of me.

I don't even know what I was thinking, offering to sex her up. I can't even blame that on the bear. It was all me.

But finding out she's never known pleasure—it just seemed like a goddamn travesty. The gentleman in me had to offer to right that wrong. I swear it was an act of community service, not self-interest.

Oh fuck that, who am I kidding? I've wanted to pound

into that woman since the moment I first saw her drive up the mountain. There's just something about her. That fierce determination. Her bond with her dog. The way she looked at my bear like he was a fucking unicorn or something. And that was before I saw her naked. Now I can't stop thinking about those big, beautiful breasts. Her hourglass figure, the child-bearing hips made for me to hold onto as I give it to her hard.

But I'm not doing a relationship. I have no plan to ever replace Jen as my mate, especially not with a human. So I would've just kept my hands off her.

Then she had to go and tell me she hates sex. Now I'm not gonna be able to stop thinking about fixing that problem for her.

But even if she comes out sober and still wants to tango—which I doubt she will—I don't even think I'm capable of fucking her without losing control.

I've got to get the bear locked down. And if I can't, I'd better get the hell out of this cabin. Because if I make a mistake. If I lose control, the consequences will be too great. And then I'll have no choice but to turn myself into the Tucson pack and ask Garrett to put me down for good.

Test Subject 849

"Time for your tests," I crow to the female in the cage.

"No." She huddles against the back of the dog kennel in her filthy bra and panties—the same pair she's been wearing for months. I open the door, reach in and shoot her with a muscle relaxant so she can't fight me before I pull her out.

Not that she's much of a threat against my super-human strength, but you can never be too careful.

I strap her to a gurney and withdraw her blood, mixing it with the serum before I inject it back into her. I slap her cheeks, watching her pupils for changes as the serum takes effect.

Just a few more test subjects and we'll get the right formula. We'll unlock the DNA of all shifters.

The tests on healing abilities have been inconclusive. All of the cuts and bruises I've inflicted on the subjects heal at a normal, human rate.

I require more data. A larger sample size.

If only I'd been able to take that bear shifter and her daughter, I'd have everything I need. I could've reworked my own DNA. Possibly bred her to make my own shifter offspring. But she'd shifted and attacked, and I'd killed her before I could get control.

My own fear / pain response triggers too quickly.

There must be a more satisfactory balance. One with more control. With the missing DNA filled into the sequence for complete transformation.

"Please," the female begs, but she's helpless to move.

I slap her anyway. She needs to learn to be more agree-able to my tests. Like I was when they tested me.

The only way she'll be rewarded with the upgraded DNA is through her compliance.

I slap her again, just because it satisfies me on some level. "Quiet. Your job is to remain quiet and let your blood assimilate the serum. Then we'll test your pain levels."

I turn to the female strapped down beside her. "Your turn," I say, chuckling at the acrid scent of fear that comes off her.

CHAPTER 7

 *iranda*

WHEN CALEB LEFT me on the bed with my body on fire and my confidence ruffled, I wanted to throw something at him. But it turns out he was right.

I was drunk.

And a nap helped.

I wake up a couple hours later with a much clearer head.

And then I'm afraid to leave the bedroom because I can't decide if I should be embarrassed or pissed off or grateful. Well, there's no decision, really. I'm all three.

I'm relieved to know Caleb is as much of a gentleman as I suspected. Rough-edged, grumpy, but pure chivalrous gentleman.

I glom onto that thought as I walk out and find him in the kitchen, pulling a giant rainbow trout from the oven.

"Mmm, that smells amazing."

He grunts but doesn't turn around.

"Did you catch it yourself?"

"Yep." He still hasn't looked at me. He carries the fish to the table and sets it on a trivet. Only then does he turn and wave a hand toward one of the chairs. "Come and eat."

"Thank you." I'm acutely aware of my nipples protruding through the flannel shirt. Oh hell, why is it flapping open? The memory of unbuttoning it down past my sternum comes back along with a flush of heat. I fumble with the buttons, but the way he watches my fingers only makes me blush harder.

I wonder if my clothes are out of the dryer? A bra would probably be appropriate.

I dive into the chair at the table to hide my embarrassment and pick up the fork there. Wait. He set the table?

I'm suddenly absurdly pleased that he went to the effort to cook and set the table. *In an attempt to impress his chosen female, the male embraces acts of domesticity.* Well, maybe he's not trying to impress me. If there were wine glasses out, I'd be sure he was trying to woo me, but there aren't. He's probably had enough of tipsy Miranda.

He sits down across from me and serves the fish along with baked potatoes and eyes me like a creature he doesn't completely understand, one who might say or do something outrageous at any moment.

I decide to shock him. "So when are you going to show me what a real man can do?"

He goes still, fork halfway to his mouth, lips open. I

savor his surprise. *Faced with a female who makes the first move, the male reassesses his strategy.*

The silence stretches on and I resist the urge to squirm. Most men don't like women pursuing them because they're so used to it being the other way around. They think if a woman wants them, there must be something wrong with her. Or it takes away the thrill of the hunt. I'd hoped Caleb would be more evolved, but maybe I read him wrong. His body definitely screams *macho.*

After a long moment he shrugs and says, "Well, you *are* here for research purposes." He takes a bite of food. Is there a playful gleam in his eyes?

"Right. Strictly research," I agree. "Scientific studies."

A ghost of a smile plays around his lips. "We *do* still have the whole night to kill."

"Right. And we've already played truth or dare."

His booming laugh startles me. I swear it surprises him, too, because he cuts it off immediately and blinks like he's bewildered such a sound would come out of him. I'm struck suddenly by what a likeable guy he is. What makes a naturally charming man with a babe-magnet body turn so sour and hole up in a cabin in the middle of nowhere?

What's he escaping from?

Bear looks over from the rug in front of the fire where he's been parked and wags his tail.

"Do you get lonely up here by yourself, Caleb?" I ask softly, dropping my eyes to my plate to take the intensity out of the question.

"I don't know." Again, he sounds almost surprised by his answer. "I mostly hibernate. I mean, I just sort of shut down. You're forcing me to turn back on. It will probably feel strange when you leave."

My gaze shoots up to meet his and tangles there. I'm dragged under by the depth of confusion and pain I find in his his dark brown eyes. And then I'm sure of it—Caleb the grouchy, kind mountain man is definitely lonely.

My heart tugs for him, especially because I know loneliness too, but I don't allow any sympathy to show on my face. He's way too alpha male to appreciate that. I want to ask what happened to him, because I'm certain something did—but the timing's all wrong. If I really do want this man to show me what good sex is, then I can't keep killing the mood.

He gets up and clears our plates. I gather the rest of what's left on the table, watching the wide expanse of his shoulders as he stands at the sink. He's as singular and spectacular as any natural wonder up here. One of the gems of the mountain.

I smile to myself, thinking of scientifically cataloging him. *Homo sapiens squalentum.* Yeah, that fits. *Rugged Man.*

"I'm going to take a shower," he says, clomping off toward the bathroom without looking at me. But then as he reaches the door, he turns and gives me a look.

It pins me to my spot on the floor, makes my belly flutter with excitement, my nipples get hard. There's dark promise in that gaze. *Homo sapiens squalentum.* Wicked, feral rugged man, getting clean for me. *Grooming is an essential part of the mating dance.*

The water cuts on and every cell in my body stands up

at attention. Caleb's in there, naked, getting ready to seduce me. This is happening.

Hormones flood my body. My ovaries are fanning themselves. I can practically feel them letting down eggs in pairs. *Go get some, girl,* they cheer. *It's about time!*

It *is* about time. I sincerely hope he lives up to his boasting.

Somehow, I have a feeling he will.

Caleb

HUMAN.

 Female.

 Human.

 Female.

As I stand under the spray of water, my brain and my bear go around and around. I'm trying to remind my bear that the very delectable woman in my cabin is human and; therefore, fragile. Too delicate for all the things I want to do to her. My bear wants me to do to her.

All my bear roars is, *female.* And it's with the territorial dominance of a bear in full competition. As if we were in spring mating season and he has to fight off all the other males. He's aggressive. Posturing.

And he needs to tone it the fuck down or I won't have any finesse at all with that female. I won't be able to change her opinion about men and sex. And for some unknown reason, that goal grows more and more important to me by the minute.

I fist my cock. I'd better let off some steam or I could lose control. But no, I'm too impatient. Too needy for the real thing. I can handle this. My head is on straight. I'll keep the bear down. I soap up, washing every crevice, shampooing my hair. I even consider shaving the beard, but then I discard that idea. I haven't shaved since Jen and Gretchen died. My signal to the world that I was out.

And while the numbness may have thawed these last twenty-four hours, I'm not ready to return to the living yet.

No matter how alluring that beautiful redhead out there may be.

I turn off the water and towel dry, then tug my boxers and jeans back on. I don't bother buttoning or zipping the jeans, nor do I put on a shirt.

I saw the way she looked at my tattooed chest and arms this morning. She finds them attractive, no matter what she may say about hating sex. And I want her primed. I need all the help I can get to do this right.

A whisper of the half-dead Caleb speaks from the mirror. *What are you doing with another woman?*

I look away. *Nothing. Just answering a challenge, that's all.* A male has to prove himself when challenged, right?

Nothing else.

She knows it's nothing more than sex. For research purposes.

I emerge from the steamy bathroom and find Miranda at the back door. It's illogical. I know she's not going anywhere—she can't go anywhere, but when I see her there, I close the distance between us with three long strides.

Of course she was only letting her dog out to pee. The snow-covered pup comes back in.

I clap my hand on the door and slam it shut, then pop her ass with the flat of my other palm.

She squeals and spins around.

"You're letting in the cold air." It's a stupid thing to say. I could give a shit if she lets in cold air or not—I kept the cabin toasty warm for her all day and the cold wind actually feels refreshing. No, it was more about keeping her in.

She's the hunted now.

My prey.

Her cheeks flush a charming shade of pink. "You-you can't just slap a woman's ass."

"I can't?"

"No! Not without consent," she sputters. "That's just, that's just—"

I raise a brow. My bear is unbelievably turned on by her bluster. I fucking love when she gives it back to me. She may be human, but she mates like a bear. A sow will charge a male, maybe swat him with her paw, especially if it's her first time.

The boar will rarely retaliate. He just bides his time, knowing she'll eventually give in.

"That's just unacceptable!" she finishes, breathless.

I crowd the sexy scientist against the dryer without touching her. I brace my hands on either side of her, caging her in.

"I need consent, huh?" I dip my head, get my lips close to her ear, still not touching her anywhere.

"Y-yes." Her voice drops to a near whisper.

"Tell me this, Dr. M," I rumble, breathing in her strawberries and ice cream scent. "Would you consent to me turning you around, bending you over and slapping that ass a few more times to warm it up?"

She makes a tiny sound. Her wide green eyes gaze into mine, her soft lips part. "Um…"

"Afterward, I'd spread those legs wide and lick you from behind. Lick you until you scream. Tell me, do you consent to that?"

She swallows and bobs her head. "I-I guess I'd be up for trying that."

I can't stop the feral smile from spreading across my face.

"Good girl," I murmur, dropping my hands to her waist and slowly rotating her to face the dryer. "You won't be sorry. I promise." My voice sounds thicker than usual.

"First thing we have to do is get rid of these." I hook my thumbs in the waistband of my sweatpants—the ones she's been wearing the hell out of—and slide them down over her wide hips. She kicks them off before I can squat to help her. I step into her space, pressing my hardened cock against her back as I reach around the front of her and work the buttons on the flannel. "I'm gonna need you fully naked for this."

She slides a glance over her shoulder at me. "Are you going to take off your clothes?"

I bite her ear and tug the flesh. "Do you want me to?"

"Oh my God," she moans. "You *are* good at this."

I laugh. That's twice she's made me laugh out loud. I didn't know I was capable of it anymore. "Did you doubt me?"

"Um… a little. No. Well—" I cover her mouth with my hand and use it to tip her head away from me, revealing the slender column of her neck. I drag my mouth down it, stopping to bite the flesh where neck meets shoulder.

"Oh." The little surprised syllable makes my cock surge painfully against my jeans.

I love her inexperience. Or lack of good experience. It means everything I do is a first. The heady sense of power that brings settles my bear a little more. I can do this. I'm not going to hurt her. I'm definitely going to make this good for her.

I reach my other hand between her legs. I already knew by her scent she was aroused, but the slick nectar there is even more copious than I imagined. Heavenly. I drag my index finger through it slowly, then bring it to my mouth to taste. "You taste so good, Doctor."

"I-I do? Is that a real thing? You can't really think so."

"No?" I give her ass a slap and she shrieks. "I really do." I tug her hips backward and kick her feet wider. "Now push that ass out for your spanking."

I love the sound of air whooshing across her lips as she gasps and complies.

"I can't believe this is a thing, either." She gives a nervous laugh.

I pop her ass. "Oh, it's definitely a thing. And you're definitely gonna like it." I smack the other cheek. I keep it light but firm. Just enough to make a loud sound, not so much that it hurts. I don't let myself forget she's a delicate human. Although she doesn't feel delicate under my hands at the moment. She feels lush and soft, and perfect to drive into hard.

I loop one arm around her waist to steady her hips and stand at her side. "You have this coming, you know," I tell her as I begin a slow but steady rhythm of slaps on her ass.

"N-no, I don't!" she protests, her indignation weakened by breathlessness.

"Oh, you definitely do." I continue to apply firm spanks to her lower buttocks. "Getting caught in that storm. Making me climb in a sleeping bag naked with you."

"You liked that part," she accuses between gasps.

"Fucking torture." I give a harder spank to punish her for making me suffer.

The little whimper she makes lets me know she's feeling that same anguish, so I drop to my knees and push her ass open. Her pussy glistens like a dainty pink Cinderella heart, just waiting to be wooed.

I give it my best. I tease her folds with the tip of my tongue, penetrate her, lick all the way to her anus and rim her until she shakes and squeals.

"C-Caleb," she warbles.

"Yeah, babygirl? Are you enjoying yourself yet?"

"Ohmygod, yes. Caleb—oh!" The thick lust in her voice, the ratcheted need makes my bear lurch to the surface, but I push him back.

"Turn around," I command and grip her waist. "Up." I forget to hide my shifter strength, lifting her easily to sit on the dryer. Her eyes widen and I realize my mistake, but I shove her knees wide and make her forget.

I drag her ass to the edge and treat her to my tongue at a different angle, screwing one finger into her as I flick her clit.

She sobs with pleasure, gripping my hair and knotting her fingers around the strands. Her enthusiasm feeds my desire to pleasure her. I add a second finger, then withdraw them and add some saliva to work my middle finger into her ass.

"Wait... what—" Surprise tinges her moans. But then I'm in. She shakes and shivers, her pleasure overriding her protests. I shove my thumb in her pussy and fuck both holes at once, slow at first, then harder. Faster.

Her cries grow louder.

Alarm flickers over her face. Her full breasts bounce. "Oh my God. Oh my God. Please. Oh Caleb!"

She comes.

It's even more spectacular than I imagined, the shocked ecstasy in her expression breathtaking.

I keep finger-fucking her until her pussy stops clenching, her thighs stop gripping.

She falls back on her hands behind her, panting. "Holy shit."

I try to keep the smugness off my face. "Not bad, right?"

A laugh tumbles from her lips. I ease my fingers from her and tug her off the dryer, her legs straddling my waist. "That's just my warm up."

She weaves her fingers into my hair. "Conceited man."

Miranda

HOLY MOUNTAIN MAN. Peel me off the face of the moon, because I'm still up there, a limp dishrag of floaty goodness. Pleasure still reverberates everywhere, but especially between my legs, my lady parts lit up and doing the Charleston to celebrate the glory of my first decent orgasm.

Ever.

I don't even have much luck masturbating.

But Caleb played my body like a musician making love to his instrument.

He carries me into his bedroom and drops me onto a giant iron four-post bed. "I'll be right back," he murmurs, and I hear him running the sink in the bathroom, probably washing his hands.

A giddy excitement builds in my core as I realize there might be more to come. After all, he hasn't been satisfied yet. Will he want me to suck him off?

It's generally my least favorite thing to do, but for some reason, it feels different with him. Maybe because he just gave me the best orgasm of my life. When he comes back to the bedroom, his eyes glow bright. They're not as dark as usual, appearing almost amber in color. He gives an animalistic growl and climbs up onto the bed, hooking his hands under my thighs and spreading me open.

A long lick and he settles between my legs, tongue working its magic again. Holy hell. Seriously? More cunnilingus? I'm not sure I can stand any more. My clit is so freaking sensitive now. Oh God, but it feels so good. I writhe on the bed beneath Caleb, his mustache and beard rubbing my skin raw as his tongue does wicked things to my lady parts. Heat reignites in my core, pours through my body. I pinch my own nipples—something I've never done before—and arch on the bed, wanton sounds spilling from my lips.

"Baby, you sound so good when I get you purring," Caleb rumbles.

I reach for his head and push my dripping pussy into his face, needing even more. He chuckles and pulls away, and I nearly weep for the loss of him. He catches my wrists, pinning them in one of his large palms. "Doctor, you are so far from running this show."

My brain scrambles, trying to decipher his meaning. I lick my lips. "So y-you're one of those guys who has to be in charge?" The warble in my voice nullifies any challenge I meant to infuse in my words.

His smile is wicked. Knowing. He climbs up a bit and pins my wrists above my head. "Interlace your fingers, Doctor."

I freaking love that he calls me *Doctor.* "Wh-why?"

He rolls my nipple between his finger and thumb. I feel it between my legs. "You wanna see what else I can do?"

Yep, he pretty much has me as his slave now. I'd do anything to find out what else he can do. Even if it's totally demeaning.

I stare up at him. I've never felt so vulnerable in my life, and yet I also feel perfectly safe. Protected, even. I nod and slowly twine my fingers together.

"Now you keep those hands on your head, Doctor. If

they come off, you're going to get another spanking." The wicked twist of his lips is so sexy.

Caleb, you kinky bastard! He's like a different man—all traces of grumpiness gone, replaced by dark seduction.

He tangles his fingers over mine on top of my head and nudges my face to the side to expose my neck. He drags his open mouth down the column of my neck to my shoulder, where he gently bites me. Then his tongue makes a reappearance, dragging along my collarbone to the hollow of my throat, then between my breasts.

I rock my hips against nothing, growing desperate for more. For a release. For all of it. He grazes my right nipple with his teeth and I jerk, but he immediately laves away the sting with his tongue.

My body trembles, eager for more, desperate to know what comes next. He takes his time, moving to the next nipple, sucking, kissing, nipping.

I want to reach for him—not with any conscious plan —just to participate, to connect, but I remember in time not to untangle my fingers.

"Caleb, I can't stand it," I sob. "Please."

He sits back on his heels and strums my clit idly with his thumb. "What's the matter, Doctor? You need to come again?"

I nod quickly. "Yes." I look down at the bulge in his jeans. "Are you going to, um…"

He gives his cock a squeeze through his jeans, but he shakes his head. "I don't have any condoms."

I can't describe the sense of desperation that rips through me. "What?"

Oh.

I appreciate his honesty and concern.

I lick my lips again—damn, I have to break that habit. "Well, I'm on the pill. Just to regulate my periods. So, um, if you wanted to... I mean, I'm clean. Are you clean?"

His eyes glow. I mean, I swear, they actually glow. Like a cat's eyes at night.

"I'm clean." His voice is rough and gravelly. "You sure? I mean, you missed your pill today."

"I'll take two tomorrow. It will be all right." This is totally a first. Me being the one to beg for sex. Trying to convince my partner instead of the other way around.

Caleb locks his gaze on mine as he squeezes his cock through his jeans. His body is lean and powerful. A beautiful mass of inked muscle.

A shiver of excitement goes through me.

This is happening.

With Caleb, the extremely hot, soon-to-be-naked ripped mountain man.

"Roll over."

"What?" I arch my brows in surprise.

"You heard me. I want to fuck you from behind. You can let go of your fingers now."

"I want to watch you undress first," I say stubbornly.

He gives me a crooked smile. "Are we bargaining? I thought I was in charge, here."

"*You thought* being the operative words," I throw back at him. But then I lose all focus on conversation because I realize his jeans are open, the front of his boxers straining to conceal what I'm so desperate to see.

Oh holy hell. It's as big as I suspected! Huge, really. He shucks the jeans and boxers.

A little thread of fear twists in me. "I'm not sure that's going to fit." My voice sounds small.

"Oh it'll fit. And you'll like it. Now roll over."

Ooh. That bossy thing really does something to me. Makes my core turn molten, heat pour down my inner thighs. It makes my toes curl. I roll to my belly, and turn to look over my shoulder to watch him. I don't want to miss a single second of this.

He smiles. "Good girl." He climbs onto the bed. "Open for me."

I can only assume he means my legs, so I part my thighs, spreading my ankles wide on the bed.

"Mmm," he growls. "Beautiful. That's fucking beautiful."

I do feel beautiful. I feel sexy and desirable. Three things I never, ever feel. My big breasts may get ogled a lot, but all it usually inspires is shame in me. Frustration or anger on a stronger day.

No, right now I'm receiving his praise in a whole new way. Believing it. Reveling in it.

He kneels between my legs and nudges them even wider with his knees. "Do you know how beautiful you are?"

He keeps saying it. *Beautiful.*

"I feel beautiful right now," I say in no more than a whisper.

He grasps my wrists and pins them over my head, much like he did when I was on my back. He lowers his head to mine, his breath feathering across my ear. "You'd better *believe* you're beautiful. If you don't, you have another lesson coming."

Another lesson.

I have no idea what that means, but it sounds dirty and tantalizing and everything I'd love.

"Now you're going to take my big cock because you know I'm gonna use it right." He nudges my entrance with the tip. It feels so good to feel him unsheathed, his velvety steel rubbing in my juices.

I want it in me.

So badly.

I arch my ass up, push against him.

He chuckles as the tip slides inside me.

I moan.

He eases in with steady pressure. One inch. Another. I force my muscles to relax. I'm so wet down there, he slides in like he was made for me. Or like I was made for him.

It feels heavenly. Freaking perfect. All that tongue action was great, but nothing replaces a cock. Not even fingers or any vibrator I've tried. No, this is the satisfaction I've been craving. This is what I need. Even as his large manhood stretches me wide, fills me too full, the pleasure overtakes all fear.

He keeps pushing until his loins hit my ass and then he scythes in and out, bumping my ass with each instroke.

I've never had a guy turn me around and take me from behind before—okay, I realize now how limited my experience really was—but I love the position. Each bump of my ass stimulates me even more. He's in deep, but it doesn't hurt; it just feels right.

"Yes," I moan. "More."

"Oh, I'll give you more." The dark promise is followed

by a hand dropping to my nape, holding me in place as he starts to pound into me harder.

Faster.

The room echoes with wanton wailing—I guess it's coming from me, but I don't know because I'm completely losing my mind.

I try to form words, but only gibberish spills from my lips.

It goes on and on, every satisfying stroke driving me into a deeper frenzy. I don't want it to ever stop, and yet I need it to come to its natural conclusion with such total desperation I'm clawing at the bedcover.

"Yes, please, yes," I chant and he slams in even harder, his loins slapping my ass like an erotic spanking.

Caleb lets out a low rumble—a bestial sound and then a louder roar just before he plunges deep and comes.

I scream out my approval, my internal muscles clamping around his cock, squeezing and milking it for all it's worth. I swear I feel the heat of his cum searing me. Fireworks explode behind my eyes. I've never felt so feminine. Been able to receive so much pleasure. Known the throes of passion.

Caleb taught me this.

My grumpy rescuer. The bearded mountain man with sculpted muscles.

Caleb pushes the hair back from my face and I turn my head to look over my shoulder at him. "You okay?"

I nod. "Definitely."

"You still think sex is overrated?"

My laugh comes out husky and raw. "Not the way you do it."

His satisfied grin makes butterflies take off in my tummy. He's so beautiful when he smiles—his teeth gleaming white, the way his eyes crinkle at the corners.

And that's when I realize—he has smile lines around his eyes. This man used to laugh and smile a lot.

So what changed?

CHAPTER 8

aleb

I SHOULD BE furious with myself. Or at least be wracked with guilt. And I do feel some of that. But mostly… mostly what I notice is how *sane* I feel.

For three years I've been tottering on the edge of insanity. I've let the bear run the show too often, lost my grip on reality. On living. On being human. I've even wondered sometimes if I was responsible for what happened to Jen and Gretchen. They were killed by bear claws, after all.

And now—after one fuck with a young human female, I'm me again. I can think straight. Clearer. My surroundings seem more in focus, the fog's lifted.

"How did that rate on your scale?" Miranda peeps up at me from under her lashes—like she took shy pills and they're suddenly taking effect. Her cheeks are flushed a pretty pink, red hair a disheveled halo around her glowing face.

I scowl, because her question makes me think of rating her against other women, which immediately brings to mind Jen.

The doctor flushes a deeper red, though, and I kick myself. Wounding her pride was never part of this. I may have had something to prove, but it wasn't about her lack of skill or appeal.

I rub a hand over my face and down my beard. "Best sex I've had in three years." That's a truth I don't have to feel guilty about.

But she's too smart. She leans up on her forearms and cocks her head to the side. "Is this the only sex you've had in three years?"

I offer a chagrined smile. "You got me there."

She sits up in the bed, her big tits shifting as she comes to vertical. She's so fucking voluptuous. So appealing. Even though I just came—and hard—my cock gets chubby again.

She notices.

There's no game playing in her next question, though. No badgering, no coyness. No judgment, either.

"Did you lose someone, Caleb?" Her voice is soft. Soothing.

A sound tumbles from my lips. A bark of some sort. Not a laugh, not a sob. Something in between. I fall down onto the bed beside her and stare at the ceiling. The vulnerability of looking in her eyes right now is too much. "I don't know how you figured that out."

"This place is clearly yours, but it has feminine

touches, too."

"Well, damn. You examined the data, didn't you? Guess that's why you have the Ph.D." I interlace my hands behind my head. I usually get pissed off—or downright rage-filled—when people want to talk about my loss. But for some reason, this conversation comes as a relief.

Like my past is a burden I've been wanting to share.

And Miranda's the perfect listener. She doesn't speak. Doesn't ask any more questions. Just offers her silence as a spacious offering. A space I can fill if I like. Or not.

"My wife and young daughter were killed a few years back."

I hear her shocked intake of breath, but still she refrains from speech. Just lets me talk.

"I found them down by the river. Bear attack. Or so the police said. Their bodies were ripped up by some kind of wild animal. I don't know—it doesn't make sense to me."

She waits a while longer before she murmurs, "I heard about the attack. It didn't make sense to me, either. I actually chalked it up to small town small-mindedness."

I turn to look at her. Her words are so welcome. Like a lifeline I can hang onto. I've felt like a crazy man for so many months now. Everyone around me, shifters included, said it had to be a bear. Shifters figure it was someone who lost control of their animal—who lost their humanity and went nuts. Kind of like what nearly happened to me after their murder.

Humans thought the bear must be rabid. Or overly aggressive.

But this highly intelligent, well-educated ecologist beside me knew the story couldn't be true. Just as I did.

She reaches out and touches my biceps with her finger-tips. "Thank you for telling me. I can't imagine how hard it must be for you."

"Don't," I cut her off. I don't want her sympathy, even if it soothes me like a balm.

"Do... do you want me to go back to my room to sleep?" It's a sweet offer and one that comes as a relief. I wouldn't have asked her to leave, but I was suddenly feeling like it was wrong to have her in this bed.

"Yeah. Maybe that would be best." My voice sounds more gruff than I mean it to and she winces.

Damn.

I catch her hand as she's rolling away from me. "Miranda?"

"Yeah?" She turns, her red hair swishing over her shoulder.

"Thanks." I let go of her hand.

She gives a surprised laugh as she gets out of the bed, then grabs one of the pillows and uses it to cover herself. "Not sure what for, but you're welcome."

"For this," I wave a hand to the bed. "And for"—I scrub my hand over my face again—"for listening."

Her brows arch in surprise. "Yeah. You're welcome. Thank you for, um, the research data."

I can't help the grin that forms at the corners of my mouth. And suddenly the desire to give her a few more data points surfaces.

Good thing she's already at the door.

"Good night, Caleb."

Wow. That sounds so familiar. So intimate.

"Good night, Doctor."

CHAPTER 9

 *aleb*

I HARDLY SLEEP AT ALL, which is unheard of for me, especially in winter. It's like my bear thinks it's summer or something. He's happy.

I mean really happy. Who knew all he needed was to bang a pretty scientist?

Even my guilt can't take away his joy.

Fuck, I'm downright chipper as I slip out of bed at the crack of dawn and start the coffee machine. A half hour later I've prepped everything necessary to make salmon, spinach and cream cheese omelets and I have potatoes and onions sautéing on the stove.

"Oh my God, it smells amazing in here."

I turn to watch Miranda's entrance. She comes out in her tank top and my sweat pants, dog trotting at her feet. She's adorably disheveled, her thick hair a mess from the hard fucking I gave her last night, her green eyes bright against cheeks flushed with sleep. It surprises me that the words that rise to my lips are *You look beautiful.*

Not appropriate by any means. I mean, not inappropriate either, but we aren't dating. We had sex as a proof of possibilities, nothing more. I can't go acting like she's my girlfriend suddenly.

That doesn't stop my cock from thickening at the way her braless breasts shift under her tank top. I'm suddenly imagining shoving that tank top up and pouring honey all over her tits, just so I can thoroughly lick it off.

She must catch my vibe, because her nipples harden and her breath catches. I catch the musk of her arousal, even across the scent of the food.

"I slept like a rock," she says with an embarrassed laugh.

"Good sex will do that to you."

"Yeah." Another chuckle. She pushes her hair out of her face. "You don't have to convince me anymore. I'm a convert. You don't possibly rent out your services or anything, do you?" She face flushes a deeper pink, like she can't believe she suggested it.

And now I'm harder than marble. "Well, I'm happy to provide you with another, you know, data set or two. I mean, for your research." My voice comes out rougher than normal.

Her nipples protrude even more.

Her lids droop. She takes two steps closer, her hands sliding up her ribs to cup her breasts.

Fuck. Me.

I'm on her in a flash. I probably moved shifter fast

without meaning to. I grab her arms and spin her around until her back hits my fridge. It rattles from the impact. My lips descend onto hers, capturing her full mouth, hell, declaring fucking *war* on it. I press my hard body right up against her soft, forgiving one, grind my erection into her belly.

She moans, clutching my biceps for dear life.

I shove my hand unceremoniously down the front of her sweatpants and cup her pussy. She's juicy wet. One finger sinks into her heat without me even trying.

She kisses me back, mouth moving frantically over my lips, tongue twining with mine.

"I'm gonna fuck you right up against this refrigerator," I growl, lifting one of her legs and placing it around my waist. "Do I need consent for that?"

"You have it," she pants and slides her hands up the inside of my shirt, pawing my pecs.

"You're beautiful." I say it now. Because it should be said. She deserves to hear it often and I get the feeling she hasn't.

I unbutton my jeans and free my cock as I twist my lips over hers in another brutal kiss. I yank her sweats to the floor, dropping to my haunches in the process and taking a long lick of her nectar.

"Oh!" Her hips jerk and loll, her bare ass making a warm print on my refrigerator.

I dismiss any notion of going slow and doing this thing properly. My bear needs to fuck her again, and she wants it, so I'm just going for gold here. I stand up and spear her with my erection.

Her green eyes widen and lift to my face. I have to

bend my knees, but I lift her leg higher, hooking it over my forearm for better access. It tips her pussy toward me and opens her like a flower. I sink into her delicious heat, drill all the way in. The refrigerator thuds against the wall, condiment jars rattle against the shelves. I love the way her surprised gaze stays glued to mine, like she doesn't want to miss anything. Or needs more of a clue about what's happening. Her innocence should make me want to be gentle and go slow, but it doesn't.

It makes me want to fucking *devour* her.

Consume her.

I'm the predator and she's my prey. My next meal.

I thrust up hard, make her breath hitch each time I slam my hips against hers, slam her ass into the fridge, the fridge into the wall. She lets out a tiny whimper and I dial it back.

"You okay, Doctor?"

"Fuck, yes," she bursts out, making me laugh.

"Good," I rumble. "Because I'm going to fuck you so hard you won't walk straight."

"I-I think you already accomplished that," she gasps, laughter and lust mingled in her melodic voice.

"You're going to take it because you know I'll make you feel good. Don't you?"

"Yes! Yes, Caleb."

I love hearing my name in those passionate tones. I find her asshole with the middle finger of the arm that's holding up her leg.

She gasps and her pussy gushes fresh lubricant.

"You'll even let me take you here when I decide to," I taunt her. I don't know why I have to trash talk, but she responds with a moan-cry that sounds like she's about to come.

"Aw, that makes you hot, doesn't it, Doctor?" I massage her anus, slap it lightly, all the while I'm fucking her so hard I'm in danger of sending the refrigerator straight through the wall to the outside. And the walls of this cabin are solid logs.

"You want me to fuck this tight little hole?" I continue to lightly slap her anus with a couple fingertips.

"Oh my *Gawd*."

Heat flushes through my body. My teeth lengthen like I want to give her a mating bite. I'd better come soon or this could end badly.

"You ready to come, Doctor? Are you gonna scream my name when you do?"

"Yes, Caleb, *yes*." I pound into her with unforgiving strokes, making sure she feels every inch of me, learns what it means to take giant shifter cock.

"Scream it," I command, fucking her into oblivion.

"Caleb, Caleb, Caleb, ohmygod, yes! Yes, Caleb!"

I shove deep and come as her walls squeeze and tighten around my manhood. My bear roars in satisfaction. Or maybe that was me. All I know is the gratification shooting through my entire body, pouring well-being through my limbs like a healing balm. My emotions soothed, my mind calmed to a state of stillness.

My vision clears and I realize I still have her pinned against the fridge, shuddering and panting, her large breasts sliding against my chest with each breath.

I let go of her leg first, but don't pull out. It changes the angle of entry, enhancing the feeling of still being seated deep inside her. Then, reluctantly, I ease out. "You okay?"

"Uh huh." She licks her lips. Her knees buckle and she gives a shaky laugh. "But I don't think I can stand."

"I'll hold you up, baby. I'm not gonna let you fall." I kiss her temple. It's an affectionate gesture—different from the raw sex we just had. It feels wrong. No, that's not true. It felt right, that's why I did it.

But I want to make it wrong. I need to make it wrong. Because I am not wooing this lovely female to be my mate. I am simply pounding out a carnal desire with her. Nothing more.

She doesn't want more.

I don't want more.

End of story.

She holds onto my arms for a moment, then Bear whines by the back door, and she gives me a gentle shove away.

I bend to pick up her sweats and hand them to her. "Hungry?"

Her smile brightens the entire kitchen. "Famished."

Miranda

HOLY SNOWBALLS. I now understand the term "the throes of passion." It's when your body takes over your brain and you'll do anything to get satisfaction.

And I definitely got satisfaction. My mountain man is a freaking *beast.*

Like serious man-beast. How could I have not thought sex was fun?

Ew, because I had the lamest partners in the history of copulation, that's how.

I yank on Caleb's sweatpants, walk to the door and pull it open for Bear, then shriek as snow tumbles in. Bear wags his tail like the snow is a friend who wants to play. It's drifted almost to the top of the door, but there are six inches of daylight there, and the sun streams right into my eyes.

There's nowhere for Bear to go, so he pees on the top step, where the overhang kept the snow from falling.

Caleb appears behind me and slaps my ass. "I guess it stopped."

"Um, how do we get out?"

His chuckle is low and sexy. "Guess we'll have to tunnel our way through it."

Oh. Wow. It sounds so fun when he says it. Like it's a game we're going to play. Right before we build snowmen and an igloo.

I shut the door and throw down the towel he used last night to soak up the snowmelt all over the floor.

Caleb's already headed to the kitchen where he washes his hands and then breaks eggs into a bowl.

I saunter over, drawn like a magnet to his body. "Whatcha making?"

"How do you feel about a salmon omelet?"

"Oh my God, are you serious? It sounds like something I'd die for."

He turns and pins with me a dark stare. "Too soon."

I laugh.

"No dying on my watch."

Warmth blooms in my chest. In my cheeks, too. I guess I'm blushing. Caleb grunts that my omelet is ready.

I take the plate from him, which is piled high with potatoes and the best-looking omelet I've ever seen. "Thank you. I'm so excited. I've never had a salmon omelet."

Caleb's eyes crinkle.

It's my new favorite thing.

I sit to eat while he returns to the stove to cook a second omelet. "So you really like fish? I would've thought a guy like you would be more of a red meat kind of man."

Caleb shrugs. "I eat red meat. But I like to fish, so I eat fish."

It's such a straightforward answer from a straightforward man. I may have found him grumpy at first, but at least he never plays games. His intentions are always clear. I like that about him.

I get up and serve myself coffee, enjoying the comfortable way he moves over and lets me in. Like I belong here. Or I'm welcome. Like we're roommates—with benefits.

That actually makes me smile.

I start humming to myself as I pour the two cups of coffee and add milk and sugar to mine. I noticed he took his black yesterday.

He sits down with his finished omelet and we eat together in a companionable silence—so different from yesterday's awkward conversation gaps.

"So do you think I'll get back to my cabin today?"

Caleb snorts. "Doubtful," he says with his mouth full of food. "Depends on how bright that sun shines today. There's a lot of snow that needs melting first. I don't think we'll manage to tunnel all the way there." His eyes crinkle again with a smirk and my heart does a little flutter.

Wow. Thirty-six hours and I'm falling in love.

No! I can't fall in love. This is just about sex. And research. And I hate men, anyway.

Except sex politics mean nothing in this cabin. There's no status or posturing or trying to prove I'm as worthy. He insists on calling me *Doctor,* for God's sake. Definitely not a man who's intimidated by my degree or intelligence.

We're just two people stuck in a cabin together.

We finish eating and I shower, then put on the clothes I was wearing when he rescued me. When I come out, I find Caleb wasn't kidding. He's already started tunneling out the front door and has cut a path about two feet wide and ten feet out. The snow walls are taller than I am. Bear barks with joy, running out into the snow and wagging his tail.

I laugh, my own joy matching his. It's like our own *Dr. Zhivago*. A beautiful winter wonderland. Caleb moves with fluid grace and apparent ease, using a shovel to toss snow a full five feet to the banks on either side. I stop and watch his muscular ass in his jeans, admire the power behind his movements.

After a minute, I touch Caleb's back. "Want me to take over?"

He's wearing a knit cap, but otherwise isn't overly bundled. I suppose shoveling is hard work. His forehead wrinkles with what appears to be incredulity and he frowns. "Ah, no, Doctor. No disrespect, but I got this." There is a touch of pompous sexism in his words, but instead of offending me, they warm me. Because I can tell he thinks giving me the shovel would be unchivalrous.

And I'm happy to let him be the man in this instance. Especially when he looks so good doing it.

"Well, thanks. Where are you heading?"

He lifts his chin. "I should hit my truck soon, unless I'm off." He looks up at the trees and back at the house. "No, the truck should be up here in ten feet or so."

"Then what?"

"Then I'm going to dig it out and see if the plow will work. It's a big truck, but I don't think I've ever plowed anything this deep."

Oh thank God. He has a plow. Of course he does. It fits the mountain man / construction crew vibe.

"And if it doesn't?" I don't know why I'm asking so many questions, but I'm so out of my element here. I'm completely at the mercy of his knowledge and expertise. I can't go anywhere unless he gets me there.

"Then I carry you back into that cabin and give you a few more lessons for your research."

My pussy squeezes. "What kind did you have in mind?"

He stops shoveling and tilts his head. "Bondage. Anal. More spanking."

It's like he lit a match and tossed it into a puddle of fuel. Heat explodes in my core, flames lick my inner thighs, my asshole, my nipples.

"Maybe some edging."

"What's that?" My voice warbles. I'm not afraid, but a tremor of nerves ripple through me.

"That's where I keep you on the brink of an orgasm but don't let you come."

"That sounds… horrible!" I complain.

"Nah. When you finally do come, it'll be so good you'll be sobbing at my feet."

My pussy clenches again and my face flushes red. It should sound egotistical. He's suggesting I would be on my knees—submissive to him. But the matter-of-fact way he presents it, makes me believe it's true. I *would* be on my knees, begging for more. And I'd probably love every minute of it.

"I-I don't think you have consent for that." I'm getting flustered, a trait I normally judge myself into oblivion for, but when Caleb's lips quirk up, my insecurities fall away.

"We'll see." He returns to shoveling.

I grab the snow from the wall beside me and form a snowball to lob at him. It strikes square in his back.

He doesn't turn around. I'm not sure he even felt it. Smothering a giggle, I ball up another one, tossing this one at the back of his head. It hits his neck.

I wince, imagining how awful it must feel to have snow fall down the back of his collar, but he only twitches a shoulder. "You must really want that spanking," he rumbles without turning or pausing in his shoveling.

Now I giggle out loud. I ball up a snowball and pitch it at his head again. I miss, but Bear chases and tries to catch it in his mouth, coming back with snowflakes falling from his lolling tongue.

"Come on, Bear, let's see what it takes to get the

mountain man to turn around," I tease, forming another snowball.

Caleb turns, amusement dancing on his face. "Baby, you throw another snowball, I'm gonna toss you in that snowdrift."

I run, launching myself at his body in an attempt to tackle him into the snow. The fact that I'm not worried about hurting him, or him freaking out about having a rather big-bodied woman fly through the air at him is a testament to just how manly I think he is.

The fact that my full weight hitting him from two feet away doesn't barrel him over is a testament to how bad-ass he truly is.

He catches me, a full laugh rumbling out of his chest as I wrap my legs around his waist and squeeze for all I'm worth. It feels amazing to be held this way. Like I weigh nothing. Like my size isn't too big, too hefty to lift. Like he's enjoying the close contact.

Bear jumps at Caleb's feet, as if this is a game he wants to play, too.

"Now you're gonna get it." His dark eyes are intent on my lips.

"Oh yeah?" I breathe.

His smile has a trace of wickedness to it. "Definitely." He starts trudging back to the cabin, carrying me like I'm as light as a kitten. "We weren't going to get out of here today, anyway. I just didn't want to break it to you yet."

Well, that's sweet.

"Thanks for trying."

"Don't thank me yet. You don't know what punishment I have in store for you."

Flutters of excitement zoom through me. I'm getting more sex than a newlywed here and it's like my whole body's coming alive. I feel sexy for the first time in my life. I want sex. I want to strut my stuff. I'm willing to open myself to a man.

And it doesn't feel scary.

Maybe I feel safe because it's short term. This little adventure is encapsulated by the time I'm snowed in here. And if it extends beyond that, it would only be the few more days I'm up in Pecos. After that, I go back to Albuquerque and he stays here. End of story.

Don't think about that part.

Caleb carries me to his bed and drops me in the middle. Bear follows, prancing around Caleb's heels until Caleb sternly tells him to leave the room and my dog immediately obeys.

"Get naked," he orders me like he ordered my dog. He shucks his jacket, shirt and boots so I have that very fine view of his tattooed chest, ripped abs and the V of muscles heading southward into his jeans.

"Excuse me?" I have to take exception to his bossiness.

"Ten seconds, sweetheart. Or there will be consequences."

Flutters in my tummy. Okay, that sounds exciting.

"What kind of consequences?"

He grins. "The spanking kind."

The flutters burst into a shower of sparks and heat cascades through my limbs. Before I even make the rational decision to obey him, I'm stripping off my clothes.

Caleb opens his dresser and pulls out a long, green sock.

I lift a brow, covering my breasts—or at least my nipples—with my forearm.

He climbs over me, with no ceremony—all business—and grasps my wrists. A tug and a few quick movements and he's tied me to his headboard with the sock.

Who knew socks had such creative uses?

I tug. I can probably slip out of it, but I don't want to. I love all the responsibility for this interlude lying squarely on his shoulders. Like the other times—he's showing me something. I don't have to perform, compete or do. My insecurities don't crop up or creep in. In fact, they all slip away because he makes me feel beautiful and desirable.

"Too bad," Caleb mutters.

"Too bad, what?"

"I was looking forward to spanking that luscious ass of yours. Guess I'll just have to settle for fucking it."

My anus contracts in response. "Um… wait. I'm not sure—"

"You're not, but I am." He uses his brusque, no-nonsense voice, but I'm almost certain if I really didn't want this, he'd stop in a heartbeat. Caleb is a gentleman at heart. I'm sure of that.

Caleb

I AM A HORNY MOTHERFUCKER. All I can think about is all the variety of ways I want to pound into this beautiful human.

She's lying on her back, her arms drawn up and bound, which makes her big, delicious tits part and lift. Her silky red hair is spread like a fan around her head. Her pussy is untrimmed, which is sexy as hell to me, because I want to be the guy who shaves it. I have this fantasy of putting her in the bath and scraping her clean of hair everywhere below her chin.

I want to show her every position in the playbook. Make sure her education with me is as thorough as it can be and she loves every second of it.

And right now that means I need lube. Lots of it, because I don't want her to be in pain when she takes my giant bear cock up the ass.

"Don't move," I tell her, which makes her snort since she can't anyway. "I'll be right back."

I grab some olive oil from the kitchen and wash my hands.

When I come back, I have to stop in the doorway and breathe deep to shove back the desire to give her a mating bite.

She's not a shifter. And I'm not claiming her.

My bear backs down because, yeah. He's as horny as I am.

Her strawberries and ice cream scent mingles with her feminine arousal, filling the room like the sweetest perfume.

"Spread your knees, baby." My voice comes out two octaves deeper than usual. I'm still in the doorway because I want to be sure I have the bear under control before I touch her.

When she drags her lower lip through her pretty white

teeth and butterflies her knees, I almost keel over from the sudden throb of my cock.

"Fuck." I stalk over to her and drop the olive oil bottle beside her so I can hook both hands under her thighs and feast between her legs.

She shrieks the moment my tongue hits her clit and then writhes against my face, making the cutest sounds as I eat her. I take my time, getting her good and swollen, her natural juices dripping onto my tongue.

When she's babbling my name urgently, I finally take a break and open the olive oil bottle.

"Ohhh, Caleb. Oh boy. I don't know…"

"You don't. But I do," I tell her. I dribble some oil onto my fingers. "Your job is to relax and take it. Mine is to make sure you enjoy it. Understand?" I rub my oiled finger over her anus, lubing it up good before I apply a little pressure. The trick is to wait a moment. There's an initial puckering and then the ring of muscles relax. I wait until they do and push in, massaging all around to lube inside.

While she's still getting used to the intrusion, I return my mouth to her pussy, treating her to the most lavish tongue-lashing I can concoct.

My girl loves it.

She moans and thrashes, her thighs crashing around my head, her feet cupping my waist like she's trying to push me off, but every time I come up for air, she pulls me back in.

I add a second finger, work to stretch her back hole, get her ready for my cock.

She moans, a needy, keening cry.

"You like having your ass fucked, don't you?"

"Jesus, Caleb. Jesus. You are so... dirty. *Ohmygod.* I need you to fuck me so badly."

I chuckle at how far we've come in such a short time.

I rub her clit with my thumb while fucking her ass, lifting my face to drink in the view. "You ready for your ass fucking?"

"No. Yes. I don't know. Maybe. I'm scared."

"Aw, baby. You don't have to be scared." I slide my fingers out of her ass and untie my sock holding her wrists. "Roll over and put that pillow under your hips." I lift my chin toward the pillow under her head.

She complies immediately, which tells me her fears aren't holding her back from giving up her anal virginity.

I dribble more olive oil into the crack of her ass and push her pale cheeks wide. "You have the best ass," I tell her. It's true. I'm definitely an ass man and hers is ample.

"I have a big ass," she says wryly.

I smack her cheek, and a red handprint blooms. "You'd better love the hell out of this ass." I slap the other cheek.

"Or what?" she laughs. "You'll spank it? I'm not sure that's showing it the love."

"Oh it is." I laugh, too. I deliver a flurry of stinging smacks, laying down a pretty blush on her pale skin. "It's definitely a show of appreciation."

She clenches her buttocks and wriggles, giggling the whole time.

"Put your hand between your legs," I tell her.

"What?"

I smack her ass hard. "*Now*, Doctor. When I give you an order, I expect you to follow it." The fresh scent of her arousal fills my nostrils, telling me I haven't gone too far. She enjoys my dominance.

Good, because I sure as hell like taking charge. I haven't taken charge of anything in three years—including my own life. I wouldn't think something so simple as showing a hot genius the benefits of sex would be the cure-all, but I sure as hell feel good.

She lifts her hips and slips her hand beneath her, curling her fingers into her juicy sex.

"Good girl. Now you keep working that pussy while I enjoy this ass."

She lets out a tiny mewl, but I see her fingers working, rubbing her swollen clit, sliding in her entrance. I free my erection and give my dick a rough yank. Fates, I'm hard for her. I pull her cheeks apart and line the head of my cock up with her back hole.

"Deep breath," I coach as I apply a little pressure.

She takes a giant inhale, like she's about to go underwater.

I chuckle. "Blow it out, baby." I gently press forward, waiting for her sphincter muscles to relax and allow me in. "Take me, Miranda. Work that pussy and let me in."

She relaxes more and I ease in. One inch, another.

Miranda vocalizes—one long vowel tone that starts and stops and starts again. I grind my teeth at the effort of holding back. Sweat gathers at my hairline but I go slow, holding my weight on my arms as I fill her and retreat.

There's something so dominant about taking her ass. It's a claiming of sorts, even though I have no right to stake any claim. No desire to, either.

Except that's a lie. The idea of me training Miranda so

she'll find another man and demand good sex should satisfy me, but it doesn't. It makes me want to follow her back to Albuquerque and rip the imaginary male's dick off.

I fuck her faster, my breath coming in pants.

Her vowel sounds shorten, voice raises.

My loins slap her ass as I plow deeper, harder. Miranda works her fingers between her legs frantically.

My balls draw up tight, heat spikes at the base of my spine. I come with a shout and a shudder.

Miranda cries out and tightens her anus around my cock.

I growl at the tight squeeze. Eventually she loosens, the muscles in her back softening, her breath slowing. I kiss her shoulder before I realize how tender the gesture is.

That we're just having sex.

But it's too late to take it back. I ease out and go to the bathroom to clean up and bring her a washcloth.

No more kisses. No cuddles. I need to watch myself. My bear's acting like I found myself a new mate, and that's not the case at all.

I will never re-mate. Especially not with a human.

CHAPTER 10

 *iranda*

THREE DAYS LOCKED in a cabin with a wild mountain man.

Three days, a wild mountain man and the hottest sex imaginable.

That's something I couldn't have predicted for this research trip. But every good thing has an end, and this bizarre chapter—or aside—is over.

After my sex education yesterday, we hung out for a while. I pulled out my tablet and we watched *The Voice* together. We slept in separate bedrooms again.

Today the sun's melted the snow enough for Caleb to get his truck out, and he says he should be able to drive me back to the research cabin.

I can't figure out how to arrange my thoughts or feelings as we leave. It's like I'm having an out-of-body experience, watching it all happen without context or reference.

As we drive back, I try to pretend I'm not a changed woman, like he didn't just rock my world with crazy rough sex and make me fall in love with a hurting but kind soul hiding behind the gruff exterior.

"Well, thanks," I murmur when the pickup truck pulls up behind my Subaru, which is completely covered in snow. "For everything."

Caleb cuts the engine and opens his door, like he's going to come in with me.

Okay, I didn't expect that, but we haven't really defined what happens next.

Bear barrels past Caleb, leaping out and rushing off to sniff things. Caleb puts his nose in the air and sniffs, too, eyes scanning the perimeter of the cabin.

"What?"

"Just making sure no one's been around here."

My mouth falls open in surprise, but I look, too. There aren't any footprints in the snow—everything appears undisturbed.

"Because of the missing women?"

He gives a single, curt nod. His brows are down, mouth drawn up tight. This is the man I first met. Unsmiling. Serious. Taciturn.

I wonder if he thinks there's some connection between the missing women and his wife's death. Surely not.

"I don't like you staying here alone." Somehow the sentiment sounds so different coming from him than it did from the convenience store guy. So much more personal. His concern for me fills my chest like liquid warmth.

"Thanks, but we'll be okay." I look down at Bear.

"I don't suppose there's a landline in that hut."

"No." I'd noticed he doesn't have a landline either. I guess he likes being permanently disconnected.

"If anyone shows up here for any reason, I want you to get in your car and drive to my cabin. Understand?"

It's on the tip of my tongue to argue, but Caleb looks so grumpy, I just nod. "Okay, thanks."

His mouth tightens even more, the lines between his brows deepen.

I don't know how I pictured our goodbye going—a hug, a handshake. A discussion on why we won't exchange numbers for further contact. But it wasn't this.

Caleb stalks back to his truck, the grouchy mountain man fully returned. He gets in and starts the engine, still surveying the research cabin with a frown.

And that's it.

He drives away.

No hug, kiss or handshake. No *thanks for the memories*. Not even a *nice to meet you*.

I realize as he's driving away I should have stopped him—to thank him for saving my life. And for changing my mind about sex. It even occurs to me to run after the truck and wave it down.

But I don't.

I don't move.

My boots stay rooted to the snow and I just watch the truck drive away, somehow seeming as prickly as its owner.

Well, damn.

I didn't expect to feel so much loss.

As the truck disappears down the road, it's like it took

one of my organs with it. Some vital thing from the center of my chest. The emptiness feels near fatal.

Don't be so dramatic—it was just sex.

It was *just. Sex.*

Tears prick my eyes. I didn't want more. I didn't even want sex. But now that I've experienced it Caleb-style— now that I've experienced *Caleb*—my solitary existence with Bear feels so shallow.

What am I doing? Working my ass off to prove myself to a bunch of men who will never see me as their equal because I have a pair of tits? And will my efforts ever be enough? Will I ever receive the recognition I desire? Or is there something more to life?

I look around me at the snow sparkling on the pine trees, at my feet. The air is crisp and fresh. The smell of the forest creates a physiological change in me. My breath slows. Muscles relax. Awareness expands out beyond the tiny sphere of my body. This forest, this mountain, this beautiful nature is the meaning behind all my work.

Sometimes I forget that. Research on climate change is about providing scientific analysis to the naysayers. Working on the ground level to create more consciousness about the situation. It's not about me getting a tenured position at the university. It's not about whose name goes first on a research paper, although it *is* about making sure that research gets published.

But also, it's about balance. Taking time to breathe and enjoy the incredible nature we still have on this beautiful planet.

And why does that make me wish I had someone to

enjoy it with? Someone human. And male. And sexy as hell in jeans and tattoos.

Caleb.

I sigh.

I sort of hate the way things ended.

Maybe I'll drive back to his cabin to properly thank him before I leave the mountain.

Yes. That thought cheers me. Maybe I'll bake him cookies as a thank you. Or blueberry muffins.

Bear gallops past me, tail wagging.

I pack a snowball, tossing it for him. He races and catches it, but of course, it falls apart in his mouth. I laugh, ignoring the errant wish that Caleb was here to have a snowball fight with.

I have the forest. I have Bear.

And I'm going to make Caleb blueberry muffins. And then I'll have to figure out how to fill the new gap he made in my life.

But I can do it. I'm good at giving my brain a chew toy. A problem to work out while I take the rests of my samples.

I go inside and change my clothes. And then there's nothing else to do but get back outside and finish gathering my tree ring samples.

TEST Subject 849

HUMAN FEMALE.

She's back. I saw her pass in the truck owned by the bear. Saw him leaving alone.

That means she's alone. Alone with the canine. I should've killed that dog when he caught my scent in the woods. I won't make that mistake again.

Today I'll pick her up. Maybe she's been impregnated by the bear.

That would give me immense opportunities for research.

Shifter-human genetic mix. I should get the bear to perform mating studies like they did with those lions.

No, too dangerous.

The bear could arrest my research like the lion did.

Like the lion did when he let everyone out.

Let me out.

Let me out to suffer.

That lion should be stopped. What was his name?

Nash. Nash the lion.

He's a lion like I was supposed to be a bear.

But something went wrong.

Terribly wrong.

And now I'm nothing. Not human. Not bear.

The research must continue. I must find the cure.

∾

Caleb

. . .

IF THERE WERE a pill for slipping back into hibernation— real bear hibernation, not just shifter low gear—I'd take it right now.

Forget everything that happened over the past fifty-six hours and sleep it off.

No, that's not true.

My body feels great. The bear feels great. Alert. Alive. Ready to romp. It's just the human side of me that wants to crawl back in a hole and cover my head.

And that's because of the heaviness in the pit of my stomach over leaving Miranda at that cabin. The guilt over not wanting to leave her and the overriding protectiveness that makes me think she's unsafe there by herself.

If I could sort out this tangled ball of emotion, I'd say it's one part guilt over cheating on the memory of Jen, and one part missing the quirky scientist who just fearlessly surrendered the use of her body to me and then walked away. And two parts worry for her safety.

I'm back to where I started when I saw her drive up. Needing to make sure no other female goes missing from my woods. Especially not that one.

I will fucking tear this forest apart if anything happens to that one.

I would never recover.

The metallic taste of fear fills my mouth.

It's not real. The threat isn't real. You're overreacting because of what happened to Jen and Gretchen.

But the threat is real.

Three human women gone. Their bodies still unre-covered.

A snarl fills my pickup and my vision sharpens like I'm about to shift.

Well, maybe a run in bear form would take the edge off.

I could sniff around and make sure there's nothing evil lurking out there. Patrol the area where Miranda will be working. I could easily guard her in bear form. My fur is warm and my energy is abundant now that I'm fully wakened.

I park my pickup at my cabin and go inside to strip off my clothes. My skin prickles, flesh turns hot in anticipation of the shift. My bear's raring to go.

Then go. Let's go.

I can't wait, either.

I need to get back to Miranda. Get close enough to smell her. Know she's safe. I step out onto my porch in my bare feet and pull the door closed. In a flash I'm on all fours, loping through the trees. Over the crest of the mountain and around to the river.

I need to find Miranda.

I find the area she'd told me she was collecting samples in. Recognize her footprints and her scent, along with her dog's.

And then I catch a scent that sends a cattle-prod-like shock through me.

Evil.

The scent of evil. An unnatural animal musk. Strange and somehow wrong.

Exactly the same scent I caught around Jen and Gretchen's bodies.

Fuck, fuck, fuck!

I've been searching for this scent for three years, but now that I've found it, I'm paralyzed by fear. Because it's near Miranda. I bound through the trees at top speed. Bears can run faster than a race horse for short distances, and I probably move at forty miles per hour.

I skid to a stop when I catch Miranda's scent, but not the scent of evil.

Which one do I follow? Charging at Miranda as my full, nine-foot-bear self will scare the piss out of her. But at least I would know she's safe. On the other hand, if I find the source of the evil, I can stop it forever. I won't have to play guardian to every female who enters these woods.

I circle around and retrace my steps, seeking out the scent.

There.

There it is.

Down by the river.

Fuck. It's disguising its scent in the water. Maybe that's how it eluded me all this time.

Upriver, I hear the dog bark. My ears prick in that direction, listening to the pitch of the bark.

Shit—he's frightened. I charge toward the sound, staying on the edge of the river bank and weaving in and out of the trees.

Miranda screams something.

Her dog yelps—a cry of pain.

"Bear! Bear, no! Oh my God!"

I see two things at once: the dark body of a flailing animal rushing down the river, and Miranda's running form racing along the bank in my direction.

"Bear!" The screech of fear in her voice unnerves me.

The river's running fast under the icy surface and the poor animal sweeps past me before I can decide who needs saving.

I roar and charge down the steep riverbank.

Miranda screams again.

I stop to look over my shoulder, only to realize she's screaming because of me. She thinks I'm hunting her dog.

Fuck. More lost seconds. I race on the shore until I've overtaken the dog, then dive into the water, blocking the shepherd's body from going further.

It's not easy, but I get my footing on the slippery rocks and stand, scooping the flailing dog and tossing him to the shore in one motion.

The rescue comes too late, though, because Miranda's cut down to the shore where she loses her footing. She plunges headlong into the water with a scream.

Fuck, fuck, fuck.

No.

This female is determined to die on my watch.

I bellow, my roar echoing off the banks of the river, shaking the whole damn forest.

Miranda comes up for air, scrambling to catch a fallen log before she's swept down the river.

I fight the currents to wade upstream to save her. The water's to my waist, freezing my lower limbs.

"Miranda!" At least I try to yell *Miranda.* Of course, it comes out not as words, but as another terrible bear-roar.

Her scream splits the air a second time as she clings to the log, lips blue, eyes wide with terror at my approach.

≈

Miranda

BEAR ATTACK. *Bear attack!* This bear is fuck-nuts crazy and he's coming for me.

I think of all the things you're supposed to do if you run into a bear. None of them are applicable in this situation. No one said what to do if you're in the middle of a freezing river in the winter and a crazy non-hibernating bear thinks you're a giant salmon.

I'm hyperventilating as it reaches me. I try to huddle down and play dead, but my entire body is shaking with cold and I can't protect my head or neck because I have to hang onto the log or I'll be swept downstream. My hands barely hold on. I lose my grip right as it arrives.

Maybe it's a blessing, maybe I'll sweep past the bear. Of course that probably means I'll die from the freezing water.

The bear stoops down and catches me in a smooth arc. Like snatching his dinner from the currents. His claws don't tear me, though. Nor does he bare his teeth or roar. I swear to God, he lifts me into a cradle carry and strides right out of the river. It's such a human hold, it unnerves me completely.

My heart pounds a mile a minute and I'm too stunned at first to do anything. I don't know whether to be scared or to celebrate. I've been saved from the water by a bear.

But saved for what?

Was it truly a rescue or am I his prey? I regain my wits and try to squirm out of the bear's arms, but it tightens the grip, snorts and turns amber eyes on me.

I freeze. Its black nose is centimeters from mine. Breath is hot against my cheek.

I'm not sure I'm breathing. I will myself to become invisible.

But then I forget my fears for my own safety. "Bear!" I catch sight of my dog running toward us, tail tucked, body slinking from the wet and cold. "Oh my baby puppy. Are you okay? Thank God, you're okay."

And then it hits me like a bat over the head. The bear —the real bear, not my dog—saved Bear. He saved Bear and then he saved me.

This bear isn't crazy. It's highly intelligent. And it's lumbering fairly fast on two legs.

I go still, awed by what's taking place. This incredible giant black bear chose to rescue a human and a dog from their deaths. I feel like I'm witnessing one of those rare wildlife scenes—like when elephants are caught on video picking up trash with their trunks.

The bear walks clumsily on, not putting me down. My dog follows, keeping a wide distance and not challenging the bear.

Prickles of excitement fill me. Fear too, but I'm too fascinated by this bear. By this miracle. I truly feel like it's a sign. About my life, my future. I'm a scientist, but it feels like Mother Nature is blessing me right now because I renewed my commitment to save the Earth.

And then things get even weirder.

Because I realize the bear is lumbering straight for my research cabin.

What. The Actual. Fuck?

It dumps me on my feet right in front of the door and

crowds me against the door, his breath hot on my neck. Shivers run up and down my back.

"Don't freak out."

I scream. Nearly pee my pants.

I whirl to find Caleb right behind me, his hand on the doorknob. *And he's buck… Naked.*

He pushes the door open and hustles me in. Bear rushes in behind me. "Don't freak out, Miranda."

"Freaking," I croak. "Totally freaking."

Where did the bear go? Am I hallucinating? Are visions an effect of hypothermia?

"You gotta stop trying to die on my watch," he mutters.

"Wh-wh-where's the bear? Did you see a bear?"

"Yeah. I'm the bear. I'm a shifter. Okay? Let's get you in the shower. Tell me they have warm water in this place." He hustles me toward the bathroom. Did I mention he's buck naked? And his cock is at full mast.

"Um. They do. Wh-what's a shifter?"

He's all business, yanking the shower curtain open and turning the water all the way to hot. I work to get out of my soaked boots and socks.

"Like a werewolf. Only a bear. Dog, come here."

"His name is Bear—" I break off when I realize how ridiculous that must seem to Caleb. *Who apparently is a bear.* I start giggling.

The salmon and trout. The blueberries. The honey. Hibernating for winter.

Caleb is a bear!

No, this can't be. I'm totally hallucinating.

My dog obeys him and now I understand why. Yeah, I guess a bear outranks a dog in the natural order. I giggle some more. I'm laughing so hard I can't get my pants off. Oh, that may also be because my hands are shaking and my fingers are still numb. And I'm delirious.

The hypothermia must've really set in, because I thought Caleb was a *bear*. A giant black bear that picked me up out of the icy Pecos River.

Caleb scoots Bear under the spray of water then turns to help me get my wet clothes off.

"I thought you were a bear," I giggle. "When you rescued me."

Caleb frowns. "You're losing your shit, Doctor. I told you not to flip out."

I stop laughing and blink at him. "Is this really happening? You're a bear?"

He purses his lips, but nods.

"So when the moon is full…" I raise my brows at him.

"No, that full moon thing is bullshit. We shift at will. And we don't hunt humans when we're in our animal form. Or ever."

I gape in shock but my hands reach out to touch his sculpted chest. Like I'm verifying he still feels like a man. I brush my fingertips over the taut muscles, the tattoos. He catches the back of my head in his huge palm.

"A bear?" I whisper, still not believing, even though I saw it with my own eyes.

His expression is still tight, gaze more of a glower. "Are you scared?"

I shake my head, my wet hair throwing out freezing droplets of water. "Entranced," I murmur. A more violent shiver overtakes my body, so he releases me and hustles me under the shower water. I gasp at the burn of the warm water on my frozen skin.

"Out, dog." He snaps his fingers and Bear slinks out, head bowed low in submission. Caleb rubs Bear with a towel.

"Shouldn't you come in, too?"

He doesn't answer at first. He's still busy rubbing Bear down. I watch through the gap in the shower curtain. When he gives Bear extra loving, rubbing the sides of his face and ears, my heart melts.

"If I come in there, you're gonna get fucked hard," he rumbles after a moment.

"Um, yeah, I kinda noticed your, um…"

He rips the shower curtain open and steps in. Yep, his cock is still sky high. Thick, veined and beautiful.

I don't think; I just drop to my knees and take hold of it.

Caleb sucks in a heavy breath and leans his hand against the tile. "You like giving head?" His voice is so thick I have to work to decipher the words.

I put my lips around the tip of his cock and swirl my tongue underneath. "Not usually," I say when I come off. "But it's not every day a man-bear saves my dog and pulls me from an icy river before I die a horrible cold death." I wrap my lips again and take him deeper this time.

It's true, I've never liked giving head. I always found it kinda gross, but right now it's hot as hell and I'm so ready to give to this man who's done so much for me. I take him deeper and deeper, playing with how far I can go before he hits the back of my throat.

God, I guess with my past partners and relationships, I

was so busy putting up walls and defenses to shield from getting hurt, I never was able to give. With Caleb, there's no expectations. On either side. It's like we can just *be* with each other. Open up and receive and give without worrying about what comes next.

And *holy shit, he's a bear!* I still can't process. A million questions flit at the edges of my brain, but right now all that matters is giving him pleasure. Because I'm horny as hell knowing I'm getting him off.

I go as slow as I can, try to relax my gag reflex to take him past the back of my throat. He lets out a long, long groan that echoes off the shower walls.

I cup his balls and massage them with one hand, gripping the base of his cock with the other. My jaw already aches from opening so wide, but I'm not going to stop until Caleb gets off. I need to show my appreciation fully, and this is one way I know how.

All cold vanishes from my body. Heat both infuses my skin through the warm water and pushes out from my molten core.

"Beautiful," Caleb mutters. "Fucking beautiful." He grips the back of my head and urges me faster.

My control issues rear up for a moment—like I need to fight for my sovereignty, but then I look up and see the feral need on his face. Like he's in lust-pain. Like he'll die if I don't suck harder. Go faster.

So I do. My hips buck, pussy clenches around nothing. I give it everything I have and more. Suck, bob, close my eyes and submit to the moment. It's ecstasy. Ecstasy in giving. Not even receiving.

I love it. I love every second. And when Caleb roars—

a master of the forest roar that shakes the entire cabin—I shudder with the sheer pleasure of getting him off.

He comes in my mouth—hot streams of salty essence. I wish I could say I was cool enough to swallow, but it shocks me, and I come off, gagging a bit.

Caleb chuckles. "Spit, baby."

I spit onto the shower floor and water washes it away. I laugh, wiping my mouth with the back of my hand. "Sorry. That was very uncool."

He pulls me up to stand and stamps his mouth over mine. "Are you kidding?" he breathes when he breaks the kiss. "That was the definition of cool." He kisses me again.

I melt.

Oh God. This is bad. I was totally falling in love with this man before I found out he was a bear.

And now my fascination with him just went through the roof.

Caleb

SHE KNOWS.

There was no getting around it. I had to make sure she got in and warmed up before hypothermia set in. Again.

"Listen." We step out of the shower, and I hand her a towel. "Humans aren't supposed to know about shifters."

She turns wide eyes on me. I can tell she's excited about it, which I get. She's a scientist. A naturalist. Hell, she was thrilled to see me when she thought I was a normal bear. I bet her nature-loving smarty-brain is going crazy on this.

"I will take your secret to the grave," she breathes with so much reverence I have to fight a smile.

"You have to. I never would've shown myself if your life hadn't depended on it."

The way she's staring up at me is unsettling. So much gratitude and affection wrapped up in that gaze.

And coming in her mouth barely took the edge off. My bear is riled up from almost losing her. Aggression still pours through me. Needing to get away before I throw her up against the bathroom wall and take her pussy hard and rough this time, I wrap a towel around my waist, stalk out of the bathroom and throw more fuel into the wood-burning stove. Her dog is already curled up near it, a damp bundle of fur getting warm.

"Go to the bedroom," I command. I steal a glance, expecting her to give me shit the way she usually does, but she just smiled, blushing. Like I just gave myself away.

Which I guess I did.

I can't pretend I didn't almost lost my shit when I saw her go in that river.

Fates, I thought she was dead for sure.

I stalk in after her. So much for keeping space between us. She's about to get the fucking of her lifetime.

She whirls and drops her towel, like she was expecting me. Her eyes are bright, cheeks flushed.

I advance toward her, all the fury of almost losing her rushing to the fore. She must see it in my face because she takes a step back. She still wants it, though. Her nipples are hard enough to cut glass and her arousal's been leaking since the moment we got in the cabin and she saw my extremely painful interest.

"Stop. Almost. Dying," I growl, crowding her until the bed hits her knees and she falls back. "I don't want to pull your ass from blizzards, or rivers, or blazing fires or car wrecks, or any other life-threatening situation. Understand?"

Her hands flatten on my chest, lips stretch into a smile.

"You shouldn't be smiling." I glare down at her lovely face, covering her body with my own. My towel loosens around my waist, falling away. I rip the fabric out from between us and drop my manhood into the cradle of her legs.

"What's going to happen?" She sounds breathless. Her pupils are dilated large.

"I'm gonna fuck you senseless." I wrap my hand around her throat. It's threatening, but I don't tighten my fingers. She bucks her hips, rocking her sopping slit over my dick.

I release her throat and slap one of her large breasts, making it bounce to the middle and rebound.

Her eyes widen in shock, berry lips part.

"You're going to be punished."

She lets out a low moan, rocking up again. I slap the same breast.

"First I'm going to spank your breasts. Then I'm going to spank your ass. Then I'm going to fuck you until tomorrow. Got it?"

"Okay," she says softly.

"Yeah?" My expression is still stern, but I fight a smile

at her complete surrender. I know it's not from fear. The scent of her arousal permeates the room.

I slap her other breast. "Yeah. Roll over." I lean to the right so she can roll over without tangling her legs in mine. When she's on her belly, I pull her hips into the air until she's on her knees, then cup her nape and push her torso down.

The sound of the first slap and her sharp gasp echoes through the room. I smack her again in the same spot, then deliver two more pops to the other cheek. The pink of my handprints bloom on her pale skin.

Desire rockets through me, nearly bringing my teeth down for a mating bite. Instead, I grip her hips and shove in deep without preamble.

Miranda yelps. Moans. Purrs. I glide in and out slowly a few times to make sure she's lubed up, then go for broke. I need to fuck her hard and fast. I need to release this aggression in me, work my fears for her out of my system. My fingers dig into her hips, and I completely forget how to be a good lover. There's nothing giving or gentle about this. It's pure, raw, animal fucking. I pummel into her, smacking her ass hard with my loins, balling her clit with every thrust.

The little grunts and whimpers she makes only turn me rougher, wilder. I fuck and I fuck until she's a sopping mess, until she's crying my name out with dire necessity.

"No. More. Almost. Dying," I growl, then pound in so hard, her knees slide out and we both topple forward. Her pussy clamps down on my dick as I seat deep in her and I come, my eyes rolling back in my head, teeth sharpening.

I rear back to keep from sinking my teeth into her nape

for a mating bite and spear her instead with another hard thrust.

She comes, squeezing and releasing my cock in short little sexy bursts that go on and on and on.

When my vision finally clears and my teeth retract, I drop down on top of her, my dick still buried deep, and nuzzle her neck.

"Oh my God, Caleb."

I shove my hand under her hips and rub her clit, and she comes again, choking on a sob.

Miranda

CALEB'S COME TWICE and his cock is still hard. He rolls me to my side and palms my breast, his manhood still filling me. Our panting breaths sync as he toys with my nipple, squeezing and tugging it as he rocks slowly in and out of me.

I let out a contented sigh.

Wow.

Now *that* was good sex.

I can't pretend knowing Caleb was worried about me didn't heighten the intensity. Make his roughness some form of purification. His aggression a blessing.

We lie in silence for a long time. After a while, my brain comes back online with a million questions.

"Your wife and child? Were they—"

"Shifters, yes."

"So the bear that killed them?"

"I don't know. The scent didn't match a bear shifter, but the claw marks looked like a bear's. No simple bear could've taken down my mate, though. Shifters are bigger and stronger than our simple animal counterparts. We're like super-animals."

I allow that to sink in, acutely aware of how much distress this unsolved crime caused and is still causing Caleb misery. Costing him his sanity.

"I was in Tucson last month for a fight." He pinches my nipple some more. He's rough with it, almost cruel. I never thought I'd like such treatment, but I do. I absolutely love it. "I caught a scent there that reminded me of it. Not the same—it lacked the overtones of bear. But the base smell was similar. Like it's some kind of mutated shifter. I don't know."

"But it was a human? I mean, someone in human form?"

"Yeah. Three guys. But I didn't stick around to find out more. And my phone doesn't work up here. I've been kicking myself all month for not finding out more."

"Could you drive into Pecos to call?"

Caleb pulls away from me and rolls onto his back, staring up at the ceiling. "Fuck," he mutters.

"What?"

He pulls on his beard. "I don't know what the fuck's wrong with me. I should've done that weeks ago."

I'm a little afraid to touch him since he pulled away and he's upset about his dead mate, but I lay a hand on his bulging bicep. "Stop beating yourself up. You can do it tomorrow. Tonight, if you want to."

Caleb slides a sideways glance at me. "Yeah. Yeah, I guess so." His voice is gruff. "Tomorrow." He rolls back to his side. "Miranda?" He tugs my hip to turn me to face him. "Did you see anything in the woods today?" His expression frightens me. I guess that's because I see apprehension on his face—like his worst nightmare is coming true.

I shake my head. "No, why?"

He scrubs a hand over his beard. "I scented something. What was Bear barking at?"

I consider, trying to remember the way things went down. "He ran ahead, to the river bank. I heard him barking and he didn't come when I called, which is weird for him. When I got to the river bank, I saw him fall in."

"Fall in? Did he fall in?" Caleb demands, and my heart starts beating faster. Does he think someone threw Bear in?

I gnaw on my lower lip, considering what I saw. "He tumbled in. That's what I saw, Caleb."

Caleb falls back onto the pillow. I can't decide if he's disappointed or relieved. He's quiet for a long time while I search my mind for what to say. "Sometimes I'm not sure what's real and what's PTSD," he mumbles.

"What?" I lean up on an elbow.

"I lost my shit after my family was killed. I turned into a bear and stayed that way. When that happens, you usually have to put a shifter down. It addles the mind. The human part gets lost, and the animal becomes extremely dangerous."

Tears pop into my eyes for him. For the pain he endured. I cover my mouth in horror. "I'm so sorry, Caleb."

He blinks rapidly. "Sometimes…" His voice comes out broken and raspy. "Sometimes I get confused about what happened. I wonder if I killed them."

Caleb's words hit me like a taser. For one horrible moment I feel like I'm in a horror movie, and I just realized I'm in bed with the killer. And then I know—I *know* with all certainty—he's not.

This time, I don't hesitate to touch him. I grip his arm and squeeze. "You're not." I make my words clear and strong. "Caleb." I wait until he looks at me. "You didn't kill them. Were you confused before their deaths?"

He shakes his head. "No, everything was normal then."

"Right. You're confused now because you spent too much time in bear form while you were grieving. And then you turned the confusion backward in time. That's not what happened."

He locks gazes with me, his expression intense, like I'm speaking the words that spell his salvation. "How do you know?" he croaks.

I just shake my head. "I know you. You're not a killer. You're considerate and giving and deeply human, no matter what happened in the aftermath of the tragedy. You would never, ever hurt your family. I've known you three days and I'm sure of this."

A sheen of tears fills Caleb's eyes and he throws an arm across his face.

I squeeze it. "It's okay to grieve. It's okay to be angry and to seek answers and justice. The more you do, the more you step into your humanity. Turning against yourself, holing up and being your animal, or hibernating all winter… that leads you away." I finish the last part softly, because I'm a little nervous about how he'll receive my opinion. "I'm not judging how you've grieved—not at all. I'm just saying... maybe you can honor your family by working to solve the mystery. By living."

A broken sob erupts from Caleb, and I'm shocked when he rolls into me, lets me pull him into my chest as he cries.

Tears streak my face, too, as I weep for his loss, his pain. I can't be jealous of his grief for his dead mate because, in this moment, we are one. His agony is mine. His loss, mine.

I weave my fingers into the back of his hair and massage his scalp until he's done.

I keep massaging until his breaths slow and his huge body relaxes into sleep.

CHAPTER 11

 *aleb*

I WAKE up like I've been in hibernation. It takes me a long time to figure out where the hell I am.

The research cabin.

Miranda's near-death experience.

Fates, how long did I sleep?

I stumble out of bed, only to remember I have no clothes here. Great. Hope she doesn't mind the morning wood.

I find my way to the bathroom, take a piss and rinse out my mouth with water. By that time, I realize the cabin smells delicious. Like baking sweet bread. I wrap a towel around my waist and pad out to the kitchen. Miranda is sitting behind her computer, watching me with soulful concern. The memory of what I shared with her last night comes back like a dull ache.

"G'morning," I mutter. "What day is it? I feel like I just slept for months."

"Just for a night. About sixteen hours, though. How do you feel?"

I consider. "Better." I rub my beard. "It was good to talk. I feel like I've been through the wringer, but came out the other side without so much baggage, if that makes any sense."

She lifts her intelligent green eyes to mine. "Perfect sense." She gets up and pours a cup of coffee from the pot and hands it to me. "I don't have much for food here, but I'm making you blueberry muffins. You know, for saving my life again."

I step over to her and pull her soft form against mine and kiss the top of her head. "That's sweet of you."

On the floor, her dog thumps his black furry tail at me.

"How are you, Dog?"

Bear surges to his feet and runs over to me, tail wagging.

I drop into a chair and take the dog's head into my hands, rubbing his face and praising him. "You're a good boy, aren't you? Are we friends? You're not too scared of my bear?"

Bear turns his head to lick my hand.

I lift my gaze to Miranda. "What about you? Not freaked out?"

She shakes her head. "I love it. And I promise I will never, ever breathe a word to anyone. I don't betray my friends." She stumbles over the word *friend,* and I have to shove away the silent urgings from my bear to claim her.

She's not claim-able.

She's a human.

I'm a shifter.

She has her research. Lives in Albuquerque.

I'm still grieving.

Except the sharp dagger of pain that's been between my ribs ever since Jen and Gretchen died isn't there today. It's eased to a dull ache.

Because of Miranda. And not just from her comforting me last night, although that went a long way to healing my broken soul. No, it's because of the sex and the laughter. The companionship. And yes, the friendship.

And love, my bear whispers.

Love.

Fuck. I'm not capable of love again.

No, I can't pursue this.

I clear my throat. "Thank you. That's extremely important, Miranda. I appreciate your respect for our secrecy."

"Of course."

I believe her. She'll honor me in this, I'm sure of it.

Her phone beeps and she bustles over to the oven and pulls out the muffins. My stomach rumbles.

"I hope you made more than one pan of those, because I'm gonna eat all twelve myself," I warn her.

Her laugh is musical and magical. It fills the room and lights up the corners of my soul that haven't heard laughter in years. "You go ahead. They're all for you. I'd offer to make you dinner, but I'm not really set up for entertaining here."

I pick a hot muffin out of the tin and toss it between my two hands to cool it off. "This will do. I love blueberries."

She laughs again. "I noticed. And now I know why."

I stuff half a muffin in my mouth. "Why?" I ask with my mouth full.

She rolls her eyes. "Bear food."

"Oh yeah." I give a sheepish grin and demolish the other half of the muffin while picking a second one out of the pan.

"How often do you change into a bear?" she asks, eyeing my naked torso like it's dessert. She'd better stop looking at me like that, or it's on like Donkey Kong.

I shrug. "I don't know. Once a week? Once a month? Depends on what I want to do."

"What were you doing yesterday?"

"Keeping an eye on you. When are you going to wrap this research up so I can get back to hibernating?" It's not like me to tease or joke. Hell, it's not like me to even smile, but I crack a grin so she knows I'm not a complete asshole. As much as a disruption as she's been to my life, I will miss her when she leaves.

The brightness in her face dims. "My tablet was ruined by the water so I lost all the work I did at your place. At least I didn't lose my whole pack. I was actually trying to shrug out of it before you saved me. So I still have my samples. I need another day or two to finish collecting and then I can head back." Her voice strangles at the end, like leaving gives her pause, too. I don't mean to, but I catch her eye, and the two of us lock gazes, arrested by what's unsaid between us.

"I gotta go," I blurt. "I'm going to drive into town and make that phone call we talked about. I'll find you when I'm done to make sure you're safe out there. Keep Bear close to you at all times. Closer than yesterday, understand?"

"Um… but you're naked." She glances down at the towel around my waist.

I shove another muffin in my mouth. "I'm gonna shift. Wanna watch?" I grin because I know she does. My bear is showing off now.

"Oh my God, yes." She follows me outside. I toss back one more muffin before I close my eyes and surrender to the animal within me. Thoughts scatter. The ability to think and reason decreases. My instincts sharpen. Inside my head, I'm still me, but different parts of my brain are activated. It's a little like having super powers while drunk.

I drop to all fours and lumber to the steps of the cabin, putting my front paws on the top step where Miranda stands. She draws in a sharp breath. I lift my snout to look her in the face. Her expression is no less awed than the first two times she saw me. She tentatively reaches out, but her hand freezes halfway to my head, like she's too scared to actually touch me.

I lower my head and gently butt her in the middle.

She giggles, hand landing on my head. She strokes the sides of my face, crooning softly, "My God, you're magnificent. So beautiful. So breathtaking."

I let her enjoy my bear a few more minutes, then whirl and lumber off. Her answering gasp rings in my ears as I run to my cabin.

Caleb

I DRIVE down to Pecos to get my cell phone to work.

"Caleb. What's happening?" Garrett's always had a no-nonsense way of answering the phone.

"Hey. I have a question for you, wolf." I'm not one to mince words, either.

"What is it?"

"When I was there for a fight, I caught a strange scent. Not shifter. Not human. Something different."

"Vampire?"

"No. I smelled them, too, but that scent I recognize. No, it's shifter, but no recognizable animal. More than one. A few guys."

"Ah. The three stooges."

"Excuse me?"

"Did you ever hear of Data-X?"

"No. What is it?"

"It was a government and privately funded research lab. The test subjects were shifters and humans they were trying to genetically mutate into shifters. The scent you caught is the result of their experiments. Men who were mutated into shifters. Some more successfully than others."

Prickles run over my skin. A mutant bear. Something not bear, not human. That's what I'm looking for.

"Where is this Data-X?"

"They had labs out in California and Utah. They hid them in out of the way wilderness areas. One of our pack was a prisoner there as a youth. We closed the last one down last year and freed the remaining prisoners."

"So there's a bunch of mutants running around free now?" I snap.

Garrett growls low into the phone. "I assume you're asking this for a good reason."

"Yeah, I am. That scent. That fucked up mutant scent. I smelled it on the dead bodies of my wife and kid."

Garrett curses. "Okay. Fuck. I guess that would explain it. Well, let me talk to the three stooges. They're not killers, any of them, I'm sure of that."

"Yeah, I know. Different scents. But similar."

"I will ask Parker to call you. He's the sanest of the three. He might know of some bear experiments. Or Sam, our wolf brother might, but he escaped years ago. Or Nash, a crazy fucking lion. I'll text you their numbers after I talk to them. Sound good?"

I can't describe the relief pouring through me. I know I owe Garrett my life, but honestly? I never felt that grateful to him for letting me live. Now I'm feeling the love, though. "Yeah. I really appreciate it, Garrett. Thanks."

I may be close to getting answers. Finally.

And I can't pretend this progress isn't because of Miranda. She woke me up out of my stupor. Shook me. Sent me back into the ring with my head on straight.

I'm sitting in my truck, parked in front of one the local bars wanting to show my gratitude. She made me muffins. What can I do for her?

Besides make her come ten times before sunrise, that is.

I look up and realize I'm staring right at the answer.

A large "Trivia Night Tonight" sign hangs in the bar window.

Trivia Night. Didn't Miranda say she loved Trivial Pursuit? Seems like I need to take my girl for a night on the town tonight.

And yes, I know she's not my girl.

But just for one night—probably our last—I can enjoy the company of the sexy scientist.

CHAPTER 12

M iranda

CALEB SHOWS up in the forest, not as a bear, but as a man. I'm not disappointed. I would've been thrilled with either version of him.

I stand up when I hear him coming. Bear runs to him with a happy woof and a wagging tail. "Hi."

He glances at the increment borer in my hand. "How can I help?"

I blink in surprise.

He wants to help?

What man has ever offered to help me without having something in for him?

No man other than Caleb.

And I suddenly feel like we're on a first date. Like my secret crush just showed up and I'm tongue-tied and clammy-palmed. I guess this means I've admitted I like the guy.

More than a little.

Which is a big problem.

"Well, I'm taking a sample from every tree in this plot." I show him how to take the samples from the tree and then how I wrap it up and pack it away for later studies.

He takes the borer out of my hand, all business. "I'll take the samples. You wrap them up. Point me to the next tree."

Swoon.

This man seriously has zero to gain from doing my work for me. I want to kiss him or drop to my knees and suck his cock again, but he's already taking the next sample, and then the next. He's stronger and more agile than I am. He makes the work look like a walk in the meadow. I follow along, drooling over the bulge of his muscles as he works and trying not to fawn too much.

As we work, he tells me about his phone call and what he learned from his connection in Tucson. The information certainly fits with the pieces of the puzzle Caleb already has.

We finish in a matter of hours. What would've take me another half day is done.

I should be happy, but instead, my stomach knots up.

It's time to leave Pecos and go back to Albuquerque. No more snowstorms to keep me locked in with Caleb, no more research to keep me on the mountain.

Caleb walks me back to the research cabin, doing that protective, visual sweep of the area as we go. When we arrive, he says, "Better get your shit packed and ready now, because I'm taking you out tonight."

I gape at him in surprise.

"What, like on a date?"

Caleb winces a little and my face grows warm. "Okay, not a date. I wasn't suggesting you should. I just—"

"It's trivia night at the bar. I thought I should bring my ringer down and turn the place on its head."

I don't fight the broad smile that stretches my cheeks from ear to ear. "Trivia? I love trivia!"

His lips quirk with amusement. "So you said. I want to see you in action."

My face heats again, but pleasure shoots through me, warming all my newfound pleasure zones.

JOES' Bar is an old brick building with a vintage Coors Beer sign over the door. The sign probably wasn't vintage when they put it up. More like it's been hanging there so long it's now considered an antique, and therefore, cool. I doubt Joe or—if the placement of the apostrophe is correct—Joes plural care about cool decorations. This bar is a no-nonsense watering hole where the locals go and gripe about tourists, and hope the centuries-old grime covering the building and the sign are enough to keep away any snowbirds.

My theory proves correct when I walk in and the entire bar—ninety percent male—pivots to glare at me. I hunch in my poufy ski coat, hoping I don't look too much like an outsider invading their local sanctuary. I consider waving to them all, but decide that would prove to them that I'm an out-of-towner and a dork. Instead I scuttle to the side and let them see Caleb.

The instant he walks in, the tension dissipates like it never existed. The bartender nods to Caleb like he recognizes him and Caleb raises his chin in a totally macho mountain man greeting. The move says, *I'm a loner but this is a small town, so we say hello. Polite but with the least amount of effort possible.* Lots of communication in a simple gesture. It would be interesting if we greeted each other like dogs do, sniffing each other's noses, mouths, and... other places. Okay, not interesting, awkward.

Caleb touches me and I jump.

"You okay?" he asks.

"Yeah," I whisper back. "All good."

He takes my elbow and guides me past the full tables. Trivia night must be popular. On our way to the bar, Caleb gets more mountain man greetings. A few of those eyes slide to me and Caleb's hand moves to the small of my back in another very telling gesture. Marking his territory, warning off potentially interested males. *Look, don't approach. This one's claimed.*

I could tell him that it's okay, no one's likely to hit on me, but I don't know. If there's one thing that attracts human males, it's a female whom another male, an alpha male, has claimed. Something about wanting what they can't have. It says more about their esteem of Caleb than it does about me. They see me with Caleb, and they're wondering what hidden assets I have that could attract a macho man like him. They don't know we were snowed in with nothing else to do.

Caleb gets us to the bar, still resting a large hand in the small of my back. Normally I don't go for macho *You my woman* shit, but it feels nice. Gentlemanly. Especially since half the bar (all men) are still staring at us. I tuck a strand of hair behind my ear and take inventory just in case my fly's unzipped or my underwear is showing.

I'm wearing a pink vest and white thermal, and comfy jeans. In the mirror behind the bar, I see the pink matches my cheeks which are flushed from the cold. And multiple orgasms. I feel pretty—much sexier than before I met Caleb—but that's probably not why they're staring. One, they've probably seen Caleb a few times, but never with a woman. Or with anyone he's close enough to touch and talk to. Two, I have sex hair. I did my best to brush it down, but the past seventy-two hours were filled solid with fucking, and it's going to take more than a brush to tame my "just went to bed with a raging sex fiend" hairdo. A bottle of hairspray, maybe two. And an act of God. Of course, Caleb does not have hairspray, or any "girly shit." He thought I was crazy for asking.

As for an act of God, I'm an atheist, but even I know a hot mountain man sexing me up is a miracle, and I'm unlikely to get another anytime soon.

The bartender finishes with his last customer and comes to wait on us. He's a big mountain man, not as big as Caleb, but cut from the same macho cloth. Normally I'd be scared shitless to come into a place like this, but with Caleb, the biggest badass of them all, it's kinda fun.

I lean on the bar and give the man a friendly smile. "Are Joe and Joe here?" I chirp.

The bartender raises a brow and grunts, "Who?"

"The Joes who own the bar," I say encouragingly.

"There's just one Joe."

"Oh, I didn't know. It's just the sign—" I point behind me at the door. "The apostrophe is on the outside of the 's' and that means..." I coast to a stop. The bartender is looking at me like I have two heads. The rest of the bar patrons stare at me, sipping their drinks and watching the show. I forge on. "It means it's plural. Joe and Joe. Not... um... singular but plural possessive."

"Babe," Caleb mutters. His cheek twitches in a way that I can tell he's trying not to laugh.

"Nevermind," I mumble.

"Babe," Caleb says again and hooks an arm around my shoulders, having my back in the most literally way. "Whatcha drinking?"

I squint around the bar but don't see any menus, so I cock my head and ask the bartender, "Do you have any white wine?"

Someone behind me snorts. My cheeks heat and Caleb twists. I imagine he glared whoever laughed into submission because the room goes quiet again.

"No," the bartender drawls with a WTF look on his face.

Crap. I'm not a big fan of beer. "Coors?"

The bartender takes my question as an order because he thuds two bottles down in front of us and moves on.

Okey dokey.

"Guess this isn't the place to order white wine," I mutter.

"You're probably the only one to ever walk in here and order it." Caleb grabs the beers.

"Probably."

Caleb chuckles and guides me away. My disappoint-ment lasts as long is takes for the trivia game host to stand up and announce, then have her volunteer pass out the scorecards.

"I'll scribe," I tell Caleb and fuss over the pencil, making sure it's sharp, not broken, and the eraser is good. Caleb watches with his eyes crinkled up at the sides. He thinks my fussing is cute. I know this because he tells me.

The game host calls for silence and he leans close.

"You ready?"

"I was born ready." I poise with my pencil to the score-card, eyes on the host.

He chuckles and goosebumps rise all over my body. It's nice, but it makes me want to pull him into the dim hall and smooch his brains out.

"You're distracting." I wrinkle my nose at him.

"Am I?" His lips curve, and he takes a pull of beer to hide his smile. "I'll shut up."

His strong throat works as he swallows. "That won't help," I mutter. "Not unless you put a bag over your head."

"Cute," he says again, shaking his head.

"Shhh," I focus as the questions start coming. Number one: what's the longest continuously held running sporting event in the US? *Kentucky Derby.* "And away we go…"

We fall into a rhythm, me writing, him watching over my shoulder and downing his beer. First round is all sports questions, second is television. I thank my grandma for all those afternoons she babysat me by setting me in front of her old TV and putting on reruns.

"You are good at this," Caleb murmurs, squeezing the

back of my neck. Proving, once again, that he's not intimidated by my brains or competitive nature. I flash him a smile.

"You drinking this?" He holds up my untouched beer.

I shake my head and keep scribing. I get the name of Charles Darwin's pet turtle (Harriet), the color of a giraffe's tongue (black), the location of the world's largest pyramid (not Egypt, Mexico).

"You sure about that, babe?" Caleb asks after the last one.

"Yeah." I duck close to whisper in his ear. "Most people don't know it's the largest because it's buried in a mountain."

"Gotcha." He turns his head, touches my chin to keep me still, and kisses me. He tastes like Coors. Luckily I like beer-flavored macho man just fine. The kiss deepens, and tingles shoot through my body, all the way to my toes.

Caleb breaks the kiss. I keep my neck outstretched, lips parted.

"Which South American desert is one of the driest places on Earth?" he asks.

"What?" I ask in a daze.

"Miranda, focus."

I blink but his smile is all I see.

The host repeats the question and I return to reality.

"Right." I write down *Attacama Desert* and glare at Caleb. "Distracting," I mouth at him.

"Right," he stands. "I see you got this." Caleb grabs the empty beers and goes for refills while I answer a few more questions. Amazon.com's first website address (Relentless.com), the town where mayors are chosen by picking names out of a hat (Dorset, Minnesota), and the fear of crossing bridges (gephyrophobia).

Caleb returns and peruses my work, pursing his lips at the last answer.

"Don't ask me to pronounce it," I tell him.

At my elbow is a glass of white wine.

"Caleb." I poke him in the side and point. "I thought they didn't have it ."

"They didn't, but the owner heard you asking for it and ran out and got some."

"Awww, so nice." I toast the grizzled guy behind the bar. "I shouldn't drink white wine in the cold months, but I love it."

"I'll keep you warm." He drapes an arm around me. Um, nice.

"And now for a lightning bonus round," the host announces. "Put together by our own Joe of Joes' Bar." The grizzled man takes a bow.

"They should do a round on correct punctuation," I grumble to myself.

"The category is collective nouns," the host continues.

"What the fuck are those?" someone asks, but I surreptitiously pump my fist.

"You got this?" Caleb asks.

"Oh yeah."

"What's the collective noun for buffalo?"

'Herd,' I scribble. "That was easy," I mouth to Caleb. He toasts me with a grin.

"Collective noun for chickens."

"Fuck." The table next to us isn't doing well at all. I smile to myself and fill in, 'Clutch.'

"A collective noun for fish."

'School,' I write, and turn to Caleb and add, "Or shoal."

"Lions." Easy. 'Pride.'

"Dolphins."

"Pod," Caleb whispers to me.

I nod and grin and scribe.

"Bears."

"Bears are solitary animals." I frown at Caleb.

He sets down his beer with a thunk. "A group of bears is called a sloth," he murmurs and taps the scorecard. "Write it."

I do, my mouth hanging open. "How did you know that?"

"I was bored and looked it up." He taps the scorecard again and I bend my head to get to it.

"Have you ever seen a group of bears?"

"No. We're solitary animals." He winks.

"A group of crows" is next. The scribe at the table beside us throws down his pencil. I write 'murder' and whisper to Caleb, "I learned that from a Sting song."

"Final. Buzzards."

"Yes," I hiss. I write 'committee', but second-guess myself.

"What is it?" Caleb leans close.

"This is the answer," I tap the paper, "Unless they're in flight—then they're called a kettle. When eating, they're called a wake." I gnaw my lip. "What should I put?"

"Go with your gut," Caleb advises.

"When you're ready, turn in your scorecards," the host

says and I race up to drop mine off. We're the first to turn our card in, which gives us a ten point lead.

Caleb's eyes crinkle when I return to him. He throws an arm around me, pulling me deep into his hard body and giving me another beer-flavored kiss. The tables next to us hoot and I tap out to gasp and come up for air.

"Proud of you," Caleb says, tagging my wine and handing it to me.

"Really?" I suppress a thrill. I'm sitting in a hunky man's arms, one who went out of his way to give me a great night. He's sexy, and he's not intimidated by me.

"Oh yeah, watching you get into the game... hot." This time I let the thrill roll through me. Caleb's lips hit my ear, "Only thing, babe. It was too easy. Next time we play, I'm making it more of a challenge." His free hand strokes up my inseam, and I almost drop my wine.

"Th-that sounds interesting. I'd be willing to try it."

"Mmhmm," Caleb removes his hand but not his arm. I settle back and gulp my drink. Screw Trivial Pursuit. I'll play any game with Caleb, as long as he makes the rules.

I win the prize, a plaque that says "Purveyor of Useless Knowledge." Joe himself, the proprietor, comes out to award it to me. I pick at the logo for Joes' Bar, sighing over the apostrophe placement until Joe leans in and lets me know, "I heard you earlier and yes, it's Joes', plural." I squint at him and he continues, "He was an army bud. Died in the war. We always talked about when we got out, we'd open a bar together. So the apostrophe is in the right place." He pauses. "Not that anyone gets the reference."

I give Joe a hug and turn to Caleb and bug my eyes out.

~

"A GROUP of owls is called a parliament. A group of seagulls is called a squabble. A group of sharks is called a shiver," I chant, my boots propped on Caleb's truck dash.

Caleb parks, comes around to my door and helps me out.

"A group of tigers is an ambush or streak." My feet hit the ground and Caleb lifts me in his arms. I hook one of my arms around his neck and inform him, "A group of parrots is panda... pando..." I smack my lips and try again, "Pandemonium."

"You drunk?"

"Maybe. Sorta. A group of wombats is called a wisdom."

"You're so fucking smart," he tells me and tosses me on the bed.

"You think I'm smart," I murmur happily. I watch as his coat, shirt and boots hit the floor and then he's on me.

"I know you are." He unzips my coat, vest and peels them both off. "You don't know you're smart?"

"I do," I assure him as he pulls my shirt up. "It's just easy to forget when my colleagues talk down to me."

"They're idiots," Caleb says in his macho man way before stripping my shirt over my head. "Miranda, you gotta know, you're smart and kind and beautiful. Fuck." He cups my cheek and just looks at me. Under his gaze, I try not to squirm. "So fucking beautiful."

"Caleb," I whisper, and he lowers himself on top of me. His beard brushes my neck, planting delicious, scratchy kisses down to my collarbone. "Caleb," my whisper turns into a moan, and I wriggle under him as his lips nuzzle the tops of my breasts. He tugs my bra down with his teeth and leans back to take me in. The look in his eyes is everything. I could orgasm right now, just from him looking at me. He sees me. He gets me. He cares. He always has, right from the start.

It's scary.

I turn my face away. "A group of porcupines is called a prickle."

"Miranda," he calls. His fingers, gentle on my jaw, turn my face back to him. "Is there something you want to say to me?"

Yes. I bite my lip so I don't blurt out, *I know this is temporary, but I'm falling for you.*

"Miranda?"

"A group of rhinos is called a crash," I whisper, and tighten my arms around his neck as he slides inside me. I suck in a breath. His hand cups my breasts, thumb teasing my nipple. My inner muscles tighten around him as he moves, surging deeper and deeper, hitching my leg up so he can hit places inside I've never felt before. I close my eyes, hurtling towards orgasm, mind going white. Caleb's cock hits the spot and my thoughts blank so I don't have to face the truth: This isn't forever. It's gonna end.

But not yet. Not tonight.

CHAPTER 13

M iranda

I FEEL like glass about to shatter. Everything is strange and out-of-body. Waking up with Caleb. Eating breakfast. Putting my things in the back of the Subaru.

Everything this morning has turned to ash in my mouth.

I'm leaving. Saying goodbye and driving away from Pecos.

From Caleb.

And I want to make some kind of plan—give him my number and ask him to call. Or tell him to come visit me in Albuquerque, but we both know none of those things will happen.

He belongs up here, and I have my own life. Besides, we're not in a relationship. We had sex.

A lot.

We had a lot of sex.

That doesn't mean we're a couple. It doesn't mean we made commitments or promises.

It doesn't mean we have a future.

"Well." I stand beside my car, the door open, Bear already inside, waiting with wagging tail.

"All right. Drive safe." Caleb's not looking me in the eye.

"Thanks for everything." I try opening my arms, like we're going to do a friendly hug.

Caleb doesn't move. His dark gaze pins me in place, the glower on his face stops any more meaningless words from tumbling out of my mouth.

"I care about you, Miranda," he says.

I stop breathing.

"I don't like the idea of you being pushed around by those scientists."

Oh.

We're back here again. Where we started four days ago in his cabin.

"I can take care of myself," I mutter, trying to shake off the disappointment.

"You'd better." He says it like a warning. Grumpy mountain man is back in full force this morning.

"If you're ever in Albuquerque—"

"I won't be," he cuts me off.

"Right. Okay. Well, I'm there. And, um, you'll be here." I don't mention that I may have to come back for more research. It feels like it would be fishing for something that he doesn't want to give me.

I step toward him and go onto my tiptoes to give him a peck on the cheek.

He doesn't move. Just stands like a statue. Like my kiss froze him.

"Goodbye," I whisper.

Because it really is a *goodbye*. Not a *see you later*, or *until we meet again*.

He says nothing.

My stomach is as hard as stone, I get in the Subaru and start it up. I don't start crying until I've turned the first bend.

And then I totally break down.

Caleb

I WATCH Miranda's Subaru disappear down the forest road and my bear roars in anguish.

Don't let her go.

Do *not* let her go.

But I have to. What choice do I have? She doesn't belong with me. I have nothing to offer that woman. I am a broken man, low on cash, lower on ambition. I've been broken by grief and my brain addled by my animal. Even without all that, I'm a shifter and she's human. We shouldn't mix.

I get into my truck and drive back to my cabin. All the while, my bear's going nuts. Trying to take control. Roaring beneath my skin.

Let her go, bear. We can't have her.
She's not for us.

~

Miranda

IT DIDN'T MEAN ANYTHING. Or maybe it didn't mean enough.

I wasn't enough to distract Caleb from his grief.

From his loss.

And even though I made it all about sex, he wormed his way into my heart. Because I am driving away with that organ smashed to smithereens. Pieces of it left all over that mountain.

I'm just past the town of Pecos when a man steps out in front of the car, waving his arms like he needs help.

I brake and come to stop, then roll my window down. "Yes?"

Bear goes nuts, barking from the back seat, but before I can heed the warning, the guy's hand shoots through the open window so fast I barely see it coming. He stabs my neck with something sharp.

I stare up at him, horror flushing out the grief.

Caleb was right all along. There was a killer stalking me as his prey.

And now he's got me.

I slump over the steering wheel as everything goes black.

~

WHEN I WAKE UP, I'm in my panties and tank top in a cage. It's a large, wire cage, like a big dog kennel in a dimly lit room that smells dank and earthy. Like we're in a cellar. Fear shoots through me and brings me out of my drugged haze as I remember what happened. I try to sit up and bang my head on the top of my prison.

I groan and blink my eyes, trying to get my surroundings as my brain struggles to catch up.

That's when I realize I'm not alone. There's a cage beside mine and—oh my God—there's another woman in it. She's thin and pale. Her blonde hair's a matted mess. She puts a finger to her lips in warning.

Fresh fear pumps through my veins, but my rational side is encouraged. I'm not alone. And if this woman's here, too, that means immediate death is probably not in my future. Because I'm guessing she's one of the missing hikers.

I peer into the dimly lit room and spy another cage, and another. Eight in total. Two more are occupied, also by young women. So these could be all three of the missing women.

And I just became number four.

That thought sinks like a stone, but then it's followed by hope.

Caleb will find me.

I try to shove that Disney princess hope away, because Caleb isn't looking for me. He thinks I drove away to Albuquerque, and even though I gave him my phone number before I left, we had no plans to communicate.

It's not like he'll call the cops if I don't text I got home safely.

No one will.

It will be days—maybe over a week—before someone realizes something's gone wrong. The guys at the lab and my friends will just think I'm still up here doing research. I didn't tell anyone I was headed down the mountain today.

I peer into the cage beside mine again.

Again, the woman puts her finger to her lips and shakes her head. "Quiet," she mouths.

Shivers run down my spine, but I nod my understanding.

I have to trust my fellow prisoner in this situation. She's been here longer than I have.

Nothing happens for a long time. I catalogue a million questions to ask these women when—if—I get a chance.

Finally, a door opens, bringing a shaft of light into the room, and the man who flagged me down on the road comes in. He's wearing a white lab coat.

"Ah, our newest subject is awake," he says in one of those falsely cheerful voices. "Time to start testing."

I shoot a glance at the woman next to me, and the dread on her face confirms I'm not going to like this.

My captor opens the cage. "Tell me, what were you doing with the bear?"

I'm certain then, without a doubt, this is the man who murdered Caleb's wife and child.

He grabs my arm and jams a needle into me, injecting me again. This time I don't pass out, but my muscles go slack. I can't move my limbs or even hold up my head.

The man wheels a gurney over to the cage and yanks

me out by the arm. I can't feel where he grips me, but it occurs to me he must be inhumanly strong, because he handles my dead weight with ease.

Refusing to play helpless victim, I use the only weapon available to me at the moment—my mind and my tongue. "*You're* the bear," I accuse him.

He freezes, eyes turning amber. As I watch in horror, he transforms. Or half-transforms. His face changes to bear —a snout grows where his nose was, vicious teeth stab down. His hands become giant paws, too—giant paws with killer claws. Some fur sprouts, too, but only in patches. He doesn't fully shape-shift. He's stuck somewhere in the middle: half-man, half-bear.

One of the other women in the cages screams, telling me she either hasn't seen this side of her captor before, or it's something to fear.

The guy goes nuts, slashing his claws through the air, knocking over a table and chair. He throws the gurney I'm on and my body slumps to the floor. It's probably a blessing I have no muscle control because the softness of my body makes my landing easier.

He tosses the cages around the room. The women in them scream. He continues on his rampage, tearing everything down, smashing lab equipment—decanters and test tubes and vials.

It seems to last forever. When there's nothing left to smash, he runs from the room, coughing and wheezing between roars.

I hear another door slam and then one of the women speaks. "Holy shit. What the hell was that?"

"A shape-shifter experiment gone wrong," I answer.

"A what?" This shaky query comes from another cage.

"This guy was a test subject of a government research project gone wrong. I'm guessing it made him insane as well as a monster."

"Oh lordy," the first women says. "That makes sense."

"Why?"

"He calls this cellar *the lab*. He thinks he's doing experiments on us, but they don't add up. He takes blood and shakes it up in little vials with food coloring and water. He tortures us and says it's pain tolerance tests. While we're screaming, he yells at us to shift. We had no freaking clue what he wanted or is trying to do. Only that he's fuck-nuts crazy."

I struggle to move, but my body still won't obey my brain. "I have to get us out of here," I mutter, my lips and tongue turning as numb as the rest of me.

"Yeah, good luck with that. You won't be moving for another six hours at the least."

"My name is Miranda," I tell them. "And we're going to get out of here."

"You sound pretty sure of that, Miranda," one of them says drily. "But it doesn't look to me like your plan is working so far. I'm Julia."

"I'm Rachel."

"I'm Tracy."

"I would say nice to meet you, but the circumstances are shit," I say. I'm slurring a little from the muscle relaxant. "There are Missing Person posters for all three of you all over New Mexico. You haven't been forgotten."

"Are you a cop or something?" one of them—Tracy, I think—asks.

"No. I'm an ecologist. But I met a man this week who was trying to solve your cases. He thinks this guy killed his wife and kid."

Caleb.

Thinking of never seeing him again makes my chest go corset-tight.

I can't count on him finding us. We said goodbye and he has no reason to suspect I'm not safely at home by now, curled up with my dog.

Bear!

"Have any of you seen or heard my dog?"

My heart pounds, thinking of how Bear went in that river. What if it wasn't an accident, and my captor threw him in? What if he's done something horrible to Bear?

"No." Each of them answers.

I hear a door open and the three other prisoners all make hushing sounds. I shut my mouth and heed their warning. Making the crazy man mad isn't going to be my best plan.

I need to get my brain working on a plan to get us out of here. Because staying trapped here forever as a crazy man's test subject is not an option.

Caleb

EVERYTHING in my cabin looks wrong.

Feels wrong.

It's been two days since Miranda left, and it's impossible to return to my old ways. I've changed.

She changed me.

The cabin seems empty without her. And strangely, it no longer feels like a memorial for Jen and Gretchen. Not that their memories have been erased. No, if anything, I feel more honoring of them. More determined to track down their killer and get closure. But I also get that it's time to start living again.

Holing up here alone, making myself a hermit, doesn't feel right any more.

I want more.

Need more.

Fuck, I miss Miranda. I miss the hell out of her, actually.

I look at my cell phone, where I stored her number. Of course, I can't get service from my cabin. But maybe it's worth driving into town. I can see if Parker called and send Miranda a text.

Or call her.

I need to let her know that I want to pursue something more.

Us.

I want to pursue us. I thought my heart couldn't hold another person. That loving someone else would be a betrayal to my dead mate.

What I didn't realize was that my heart had already made room for another. And I let that person drive away without me telling her. I was an idiot, but it might not be too late to fix this.

Some of the heaviness in my chest lightens.

I stand up from the couch, shove my phone in my pocket and head for the door.

And that's when I hear the whine.

It's coming from right outside my door and—

I throw open the door and drop to my haunches. "Bear!"

Miranda's dog sits and barks at me. What is he doing here?

I peer outside, but there's no sign of Miranda's Subaru. She didn't drive back here.

"Come here, boy." I reach out to pet the dog, but he backs away and barks some more. I scent his blood—not fresh. He's limping slightly. He doesn't come in, even though he looks half frozen. No, he's telling me something.

Oh fuck.

What's happened to Miranda now?

Except I already know.

I know with the certain dread that makes all my hairs stand on end. I know with the agony of a dagger through the heart.

Please don't let her be dead.

Please not like Jen.

A cold band squeezes around my chest as I grab my jacket and jog outside. "Where is she, boy? Show me where."

Bear takes off running and I realize we won't be going in my truck.

"Hold up, dog." I whistle and Bear comes back and barks again.

"Thirty seconds," I tell him, even though he can't

understand me. He'll get the gist. I dash inside and strip off my clothes, then step outside, pull the door shut and shift.

Bear whines, but takes off again and I lope beside him as we run for miles down the side of the mountain.

When I catch the mutant shifter's scent, I want to heave. I growl the whole time we run, a low, angry rumble that keeps me focused. As the scent grows stronger, the fur on my nape stands on end. And then I see it—Miranda's Subaru down in a ditch, a few hundred yards from the road to Santa Fe.

Fuck.

Bear goes crazy, barking and running around the car.

Shit. He doesn't know where she is. This must be the last place he saw her. I need to figure this out on my own.

I lift my nose in the air to find her scent. It's mingled with the mutant bear's scent, but I catch it. I follow it downhill another mile or so until we get to a cabin.

The place reeks of mutant bear. This has to be the place.

That's when I hear her scream.

Miranda

MY THROAT IS raw and hoarse from screaming. I'm strapped to the gurney with a madman standing over me. He's already taken my blood four times using dirty, unsterilized equipment. The fellow prisoners were right—there's no real science happening here. Just a delusional lunatic who thinks he's a real scientist. And enjoys inflicting pain. I scream as he shoves the needle under my thumbnail in deeper.

"Shift!" the madman shouts at me, spittle flying from his mouth. "You have bear DNA growing inside you. Use it to shift!"

I scream again.

The other women are huddled in their cages, eyes closed, ears plugged to block out the horror of my torture.

Suddenly the door comes crashing in, rent from its hinges. I hear Bear barking and the snarl of a very real bear.

Caleb.

I knew he'd come.

The madman whirls, his fake glasses falling down his face, his dirty lab coat whipping around his legs.

An answering growl comes from him—demonic and furious. He transforms into his monster self, but Caleb's already tackled him to the ground. Bear—my fearless, precious dog is circling around both of them, barking and growling.

Caleb bares his teeth and roars like a dark god coming down to smite the devil himself.

My captor fights like the madman he is, though. He has superhuman strength as well, and is totally out of control. The two animals roar and tumble around the room, smashing everything, knocking things over.

Caleb picks up my captor and throws him across the room. He hits the wall and slides down it, but is instantly up, fumbling at the lab equipment.

"Watch out for the needle!" I scream when I realize

he's grabbed one of the pre-filled hypodermics. He can't take Caleb prisoner, too. He can't.

Caleb dodges the needle and knocks it from my captor's hand. It goes rolling and Rachel reaches through her cage bars to pick it up, meeting my eye and giving me a nod.

I nod back.

Caleb tackles our captor and lets out a terrible snarl as he slashes his claws across the man's throat. A gurgling sound confirms his death. Caleb keeps slashing though, ripping open the guy's chest and belly.

"Caleb!" I scream.

He shakes his great head and swings it in my direction. His lips peel back from ferocious teeth and he bellows again, even more furious than before.

The women in the cages scream.

He seems to see them for the first time, and roars some more.

He slices his claws through the bindings holding my wrist, scratching some of my skin in the process.

I gasp but quickly mutter, "I'm okay."

He rips the other side and I'm free. I sit up and yank the needle out of my thumbnail, screaming again as I do. Bear whines at my side, licking my hand and the bloodied scrape on my wrist.

Caleb bares his teeth again, lifts his head toward the ceiling and roars his anger.

I get up to search the body of our captor for the keys to the cage, but Caleb grabs the door of one of the kennels with a huge paw and pushes his foot against the body of the cage and tears the door off from its hinges. Rachel lifts the hypodermic needle, ready to plunge it into Caleb's neck.

"No, don't!" I scream.

She freezes.

Caleb snorts and bats it out of her hand.

"It's okay. He's, um… he won't hurt us." I help her out of the kennel.

Caleb moves to the next cage, where he tears off its door, too. Then the next.

"Let's get out of here," Rachel says, rushing through the door.

Caleb plows through on all fours, knocking us out of the way, like he needs to go first.

"It's okay. He won't hurt you, I promise," I tell them, my brain already working overtime trying to figure out how to explain my pet bear to them.

We go up a set of stairs—he had been keeping us in a cellar, as I suspected. Upstairs is a crude, filthy cottage. Signs of a man barely able to take care of his personal needs.

We all rush outside, even though we're barely dressed and don't have jackets or shoes on.

I grip Caleb's furry shoulder. "Go get Caleb," I tell him firmly, shivering in the cold. We need him in man form now. We need to call the police and maybe an ambulance.

He shakes his great head, like he's unwilling to leave me.

I show him the hypodermic needle I picked up after he batted it out of Rachel's hand. "I'm pretty sure he's dead, but I'm armed, just in case."

Caleb snorts and lopes away, his great strides taking him up the side of the mountain with shocking speed.

"What. The hell. Was that?" Julia asks.

"Um, my friend Caleb has a, ah, pet bear. I mean, he's not really a pet, but they're friends. He's highly intelligent."

Julia, Rachel and Tracy all stare at me with disbelief.

Damn, I'm a terrible liar. But I promised Caleb I'd take his secret to the grave, and I intend to keep that promise.

"I don't know about you three, but I'm not sticking around here another minute," Tracy announces, walking into the snow in her bare feet.

"No, no, no," I call out. "Wait here. Caleb will come and bring help. I promise."

Tracy looks back, eyes narrowed. "Are you nuts? You told a bear to bring back your friend and you think he's going to show? You're as crazy at that guy down there." She points in the direction of the cellar.

"No, really. Did that bear just save our asses? He'll bring Caleb. Trust me."

Her lips tighten, but she comes back and the four of us go back inside because we're freezing our asses off. I find my clothing in with his dirty laundry and put it on. I don't have any luck finding the rest of their clothes, but it's okay, because Caleb's truck tears down the dirt drive and skids to a stop. He's out of the truck and running for me before I can even breathe his name.

I rush down the steps and launch into his arms.

"Caleb!" Suddenly, I'm crying. Bawling, actually. "I knew you'd come for me. I mean, I hoped you would. And you did. Thank you so much."

"Fuck, baby, fuck. I'm so glad you're alive. I'm so fucking glad." He's spinning me around slowly, my feet not touching the ground. "I never should have let you leave here. Wait—that's not what I meant." He glances up at the three women standing in the doorway. "Nevermind, I'll tell you later." He waves a beckoning arm to my fellow captives. "Get in the truck. I'll take you to the sheriff's."

My heart's still stuttering on the *I'll tell you later.* He has something to tell me? About not letting me leave?

We all squeeze into the cab of Caleb's truck—Bear included—and he drives a couple miles up the road into the town of Pecos and tears into the sheriff's building.

It's a small town, so people come out to see what all the fuss is about. Someone recognizes the women from the Missing Person posters and points and then everyone's chattering, moving in for more information as we troop into the sheriff's office.

Caleb takes my hand protectively as we go in and my heart does a full flip flop. We tell our story five or six times each to the sheriff, who calls an ambulance to take all four of us down to Santa Fe to get checked out. Caleb stays by my side the whole time, my strong silent bodyguard. The sheriff speaks to him with respect, like they go way back. Caleb tells him my dog came to get him and that's how he found us. None of us contradict him—the bear story was too fantastical, anyway.

He doesn't believe our story about the man turning into a monster, either, until Caleb and his deputies on site confirm it was true.

The rest of the night is a blur of repeating my story a

dozen times and getting checked over by doctors at the hospital.

After we left the sheriff's, Caleb took Bear up to his place, and I went in the ambulance to Santa Fe. We'd only been given bread and small rations of water for the duration of captivity and Rachel passed out by the time the ambulance arrived. She'd been there the longest—eight months. According to everyone who heard the story, we're all lucky to be alive, considering the mental state of our captor. The other women's families were contacted and the hospital is trying to keep the media out for their privacy. I'm glad I was never reported missing—maybe I can stay out of the stories.

Caleb waits with me in the hospital room. I'm sitting on the bed, he's in the chair beside it.

"Is there someone I should call? Your parents or someone else?"

"Oh, um…" Disappointment hits me like a punch to the solar plexus. For some reason, I thought I'd be going back up to Caleb's. But maybe that was the wrong assumption.

He must see my fluster, because he picks up my hand. "I'll be taking care of you tonight, of course. I just didn't want to intrude. You know, if someone else should know what's going on."

Happiness seeps back in. "Oh. No, I can worry my parents with the story later. They're going to freak out completely, but it can wait."

He nods. "Good. I'm bringing you back to my place tonight."

Contentment flows through me like an easy river. Back to Caleb's. Where I spent two of the best days of my life.

He cups my chin. "Listen, Miranda. I didn't like the way we left things."

I lick my lips. "Wh-what do you mean?" My heart is beating hella fast. I just survived being kidnapped and tortured. Talking about a relationship with Caleb shouldn't make me break out into a cold sweat, but it does.

"I mean…" He runs a hand down his beard. "I want to see you again. I don't want things to end. I know you have your career—"

"I don't want things to end, either," I blurt, then feel my face heat.

Caleb wraps a large palm around the back of my head and pulls me to stand, claiming my mouth with all the aggression of a wild animal.

I surrender happily, letting him plunder my mouth with his tongue, moaning when he drags my lower lip through his teeth.

"Then we're agreed," Caleb breathes when he breaks the kiss.

The nurse clears her throat from the doorway. "The doctor signed your release papers. You can check out at the desk."

"Great." I beam at her, taking Caleb's hand and letting him lead me out to his truck.

Caleb

. . .

MIRANDA and I need to talk but I've been too busy fucking her brains out. I had her in my bed. On the living room floor. Over the couch. Against the kitchen counter. On the bed again. She's there now, a limp rag doll, panting as she recovers.

I was gentle at first, feeling terrible about the torture she endured, and the gash I gave her with my claws. But then I lost control and had to take her roughly. In every position imaginable.

I pretty much kept her up all night. Now that I've decided I can have her, I'm ravenous. My bear wants to claim her permanently.

It's strange for a bear to get the urge to permanently mate. Even stranger that I've had it twice. Of course, I can't mate Miranda. She's not a shifter. But the fact that I want to is a delicious conundrum. I feel more alive than I have in years. Anything feels possible.

I stroke her thick red locks back from her face, marveling at how pale her skin is. The black bear and the red-haired science goddess. She's a warrior in her own right. Saving the Earth with her dogged determination to catalogue and report on climate change.

"I have to go back today," Miranda sighs.

"Yeah. About that." My throat goes dry. I don't even know what I'm asking. Or at least, I'm ambivalent about it. I want Miranda and she lives in Albuquerque. But I'm a bear and I belong in the forest.

Miranda turns big questioning greens on me.

I swallow. "I could go down with you. Make sure you get there safe and settle in."

Miranda smiles the brightest smile ever seen. "That

would be great. I would love that. You could stay as long as you wanted. I mean, if you don't need to get back here or anything."

Something releases in me and my eyes sting. I'm really going to let myself have this. Have her. I'm really going to move past my tragedy and live again.

I roll on top of her, leaning on my forearms to protect her from my full weight. "I don't like to be away from the forest, but I also don't want to be away from you."

Her breath catches, a sheen of tears glints in her eyes. "I don't want to be away from you, either." Her lips tremble.

I drop kisses across her forehead. Her temples. The bridge of her nose. "So I'll come to Albuquerque. Make you breakfast and keep you safe. We'll see how the bear does in captivity."

Tears spill from her eyes. "I don't want you to leave your home, but having you in Albuquerque would be incredible. Promise me you'll come back here as soon as you get itchy. Or you get sick of me."

I thrust my hips against hers, showing her how quickly my need for her returns. "You think I'd ever get sick of this?" I spear her with my erection and she whimpers, sore from all the sex we've had.

I take mercy on her and pull back out.

"Besides, I have a newfound interest in watching you tromp all over the competition in trivia. I'm thinking of bringing you to Burbank to compete on *Jeopardy*."

She laughs.

"I'm serious. You should be playing for the big bucks."

"Well, we can come back here on the weekends. I can

rearrange my schedule to work three day weekends. Although you may have to get WiFi. Is that a possibility?"

"If WiFi keeps you here, beautiful, I'll get it. I want you happy. And with me."

"Is it okay? For you to be with a human? I mean, is it against the rules?" She turns pink in one of those blushes I've come to love.

"It's not recommended. Yeah, kind of against the rules. I don't give a shit."

She grabs my cock and guides me back in. "You can't tease me like that and then just leave me hanging." Her sultry tone washes over me in shades of bliss.

My teeth punch out to mark her. I groan, but I can't push away the pleasure. It floods me like a powerful drug. "Miranda, I have to tell you something." It's a struggle to even form words.

She stops rocking her pelvis and looks up at me. "What is it?"

"Bears don't usually mate for life. Many are polyamorous. But sometimes they do." Heat spikes at the base of my spine, my balls are tight.

"Okaaay." She sees my teeth and her eyes widen.

"I'm having a hard time keeping my bear under control, though. He wants me to mark you as my mate."

She eyes my sharp teeth. "What does that mean?" It's no more than a whisper.

"It means a bite. A love bite. To embed my scent in you. Keep the other males away."

"Okay."

"Okay?" I didn't expect her to agree. I was just trying

to explain that I was having a hard time keeping the teeth from descending.

She nods, practically glowing.

"Baby, it could scar. It will definitely hurt." I can't stop rocking into her, can't stop my eyes from rolling back into my head in pleasure.

"Where will you do it?"

Will I do it, not *would* I do it. She's accepting this without any protests. My independent feminist wants my claiming bite.

"Oh fates." I can barely hold back now. "You tell me, baby. It's usually at the nape, but I can bite your thigh or somewhere that won't show. Fuck, Miranda, I can't hold back."

"Bite me!" She arches up, throwing those big, wondrous tits in my face.

My jaws snap and I've claimed her before I even have time to pull back. My teeth are deep into the meat of her shoulder, right in the middle of her pretty tattoo.

She screams, but I swear to fates, she also orgasms.

I come, too. *Hard.*

I've already come a half dozen times in the past twelve hours, but there seems to be no end to the essence that flows out of me now. I fill her, forcing my jaws to release and licking away the blood as I still pump into her.

She wraps her arms around me, crying a little. Laughing a little.

"I'm sorry. I'm so sorry, babe. Tell me you're okay."

"I'm okay. It hurts, but it's not that deep. I'll be okay."

"I'll let you mark me any way you want," I swear, wanting to offer something back.

She gives a watery laugh. "Yeah? Would you tattoo my name on your pec?"

"Whatever you want," I promise.

"I'm just kidding," she says softly. "All I want is you."

"You got me, baby. I'm here."

I keep licking her wound because the serum in my mouth should help it heal faster. I hope to fate it heals soon because I'm going to feel like shit every day it hurts her.

"Caleb?" Her voice is soft and tentative.

"Yeah, babe?"

"I will always honor the memory of your wife and child by your side. I don't want you to ever feel like it's not okay to talk about her or celebrate what you had."

My eyes burn and I drop my head into the crook of her neck. This woman is too much. Too good. She doesn't make me choose between past and present. "Miranda," I choke. "You are my salvation—you know that? You brought me back to life."

"You gave me me," she answers.

"What does that mean?"

"I mean, you helped me feel okay about who I am. About my body. My brains. I don't have to prove anything to you. You celebrate me just as I am."

"That's because you're already perfect," I tell her.

Her lips find my neck and she plants soft kisses there. "I love you, Caleb."

"I love you, too, babe."

EPILOGUE

M *iranda*

"Bear! Get back here!" I race up the mountain trail, rounding a boulder just in time to see the fringe of my dog's tail disappear between two trees.

He took off, barking. I hightail it after him, shivering at a little flashback of my kidnapping earlier this year. The woods are safe now

A shadow falls across me. "What did I tell you about hiking alone in these woods?"

I jerk around, leaping out of my skin until my eyes hit Caleb, stepping out from behind a tree.

"Ohmygod, Caleb, you scared the crap out of me."

With a happy growl, he moves in, picking me straight up and kissing the hell out of me. My legs wrap tight around his hips, my breasts swelling to brush against his chest. His hard, bare chest. Mmmm…

We're all tangled up with lips and tongue, Bear circling around us barking.

"Careful, pretty lady," he growls. "Not safe out here on your own."

"Why? Is there a big bad bear who might eat me?"

"Damn straight." He squeezes my ass, then gives it a healthy slap.

"The mating call of the mountain were-bear," I murmur.

"You know it."

I just moved up here permanently, and we're still in our honeymoon phase. Caleb got WiFi and I got a research grant that will allow me to live and work up here on the mountain.

Turns out leaving my colleagues and stepping out of the rat race of UNM was the best decision I ever made. I've never been so happy in my life.

"Something came for you." Caleb pulls a letter out of his back pocket.

I catch the name of the science publication I submitted to and snatch it out of his hand, ripping it open in record time.

I unfold it, skimming as fast as I can. "Yes!"

Caleb raises his brows in question.

"It's a yes! They took my paper for publication and invited me to present at the annual conference! This is huge!"

"Congratulations!" Caleb picks me up and swings me around. "You did it. I knew you would. You are amazing!"

"Thank you, thank you, thank you." I kiss his ear and temple, everywhere my lips reach.

He laughs. "What are you thanking me for?"

"Believing in me. Making me happy. This life."

He squeezes me tighter, so tight my breath leaves my chest. "Fuck, I love you, babe."

"I love you so much, Caleb."

He eases me down, twining his fingers in mine and tugging me back to the cabin.

"Where are we going?" I laugh, even though I already know the answer.

"To celebrate. Naked. All afternoon."

"Hmm…" I pretend to consider. "Yes, I think that would contribute to my research." I beam up at him, my happiness bubbling all around me.

He sweeps me up into his arms like I weigh nothing and carries me back to the cabin, where I know he'll make sure I get all the data points necessary.

THANK you for reading *Alpha's Prey*! Your reviews are madly appreciated. A couple quick notes:

— CHECK OUT *ALPHA'S BLOOD,* the next book in the series. (flip the page to read the first chapter!).

--Come meet Renee and Lee in person at Shameless Con.

WANT MORE? ALPHA'S BLOOD

Please enjoy the first chapter of *Alpha's Blood*

Selene

The stage is an old battered platform, transformed by lush red curtains and glaring spotlights. How many Macbeths have died here? How many Hamlets? I wait in the wings, listening to the murmur of the audience. Goosebumps rise up and down my arms.

Relax, my mentor's voice whispered to me. *You're going to perform splendidly.*

I certainly hope so. I've trained for this moment my whole life. I'm wearing a strappy silky dress that drapes over my breasts and hips, molding to them with a nod to modesty while leaving my legs bare below mid thigh. The revealing attire doesn't bother me, but without weapons I'm naked. Since the age of sixteen, I've always had weapons on me. I used to fall asleep cradling my favorite: a wooden stake.

This is your greatest role. Your ultimate performance.

My mentor said. *If you fail, you pay the ultimate price.* His voice deepened. *Do not fail me.*

I will not fail. After tonight, my life will hang in the balance, but that is nothing new. It always has. I've waited, and cried and sweated and fought and lived and breathed and died for this moment. The training demanded all of me, and I have given it my all. Whatever happens after tonight was plotted long ago, my part in the plot custom-made for me. I was born to play this role. Everything in my life has led to this moment.

"Ten minute warning," a black clad backstage hand calls. His gaze drifts over me like I'm a part of the set. I raise my chin and meet his eyes, staring until he drops them and scuttles away. I smooth my see through garment and uncurl my lip. Tonight I pay a submissive part, but not until the curtains rise. I won't cringe before these cockroaches. I don't even bow to my mentor. It amuses him, my show of dominance. Or perhaps he thinks my alpha strength will protect me in my final mission. Either way, he allows my cheek. I'd be dead if he didn't.

Two shadows move in the depths of the stage. I don't bother glancing back. The guards are there for my protection, and to herd me onto the stage if I get cold feet. Unnecessary. I can't wait to play this role.

This old theater is long past its use. The air is dusty, stale. The green room holds another, sour scent that only grows worse when you descend the stairs into the basement filled with cages. My mentor hustled me past them, ordering me to focus on the endgame. A part of me wanted to turn and face the cages, find the ones that were full and break the bars. Free the frightened shifters. In another life, that would be my mission. Maybe it still could be—if I survived.

Will they end up on stage? I asked as we climbed the stairs, escaping those glittering eyes.

Some of them, my mentor answered. *Some of them are waiting pickup.* He caught my anger and disgust and leaned close. *This is the perversion that Lucius Frangelico allows. When he is gone, we will right this wrong.*

It was the perfect thing to say. When I step on stage, all I will think about is the king sitting in the audience. The end of his reign will send shockwaves through his corrupt kingdom.

But first, Lucius Frangelico has to die.

He is here? Right now? I asked Xavier.

On his way, my mentor answered. *My spies report he will arrive in time. Once he is seated, we give the signal, and your part will begin.*

My fists clench at my sides and I force them to straighten. Time to get into my role. I must perform perfectly or I won't survive.

Another figure appears. An older woman emerges from the green room to give me a critical once over. I stand straight and let her study me. I even drop my eyes to the floor, acting like the submissive I'm supposed to be.

My hair is braided and pinned onto my head in a crown. I'm wearing minimal makeup: a hint of eye shadow, mascara, blush. Just enough so the lights don't wash me out, with a bold touch around my mouth: the red, red lipstick. The color of blood and vampire dreams.

You will catch his attention immediately, my mentor purred. *He will be pleased.* Xavier's eyes swept up and down my half naked form. I told myself his attention was impersonal, clinical, but couldn't help enjoying the approval glittering in his single eye.

And if he doesn't take the bait? I asked.

He will. If not tonight, one of my colleagues will purchase you and show you off. Wave you under Frangelico's nose. It is up to you to catch his attention. Xavier's large hands closed around my arms, his grip cruel and painful. His fingers left bruises, marks I accepted gratefully. My training didn't allow for comfort or friendly contact, but it left plenty of marks. I welcomed them like kisses or hugs. Pain became pleasure, and each bruise made me stronger, a honed weapon.

Xavier increased his grip, and I bit back a moan.

Good girl, he said, and my spirits soared. I wasn't sure if he meant to hurt me until he stepped back and let the makeup artist do her work. When she would cover the marks with makeup, he ordered her to leave them. *They catch the eye.* Xavier chucked me under the chin. *Remember all I've taught you.* I'd bowed my head and the one-eyed vampire walked off. The makeup artist shuddered, and I gave her a small smile of solidarity. Big, broad as a wrestler, with the ruined side of his face made barely presentable by an eye patch, Xavier was scary. He'd raised and trained me with unrelenting focus on my final goal: revenge. His methods were brutal and cruel. If he hadn't given me everything I'd need to avenge my slain pack, I'd hate him.

Maybe I do hate him. In my world, hate is an emotion not so far from love.

The makeup artist gives a brisk nod and walks off, her

heels clopping on the scarred stage. With my eyes trained on the floor, I can't escape the signs of shifters—the shed fur, the scrapes on the floor where the guards forced the shifters onto the stage. The shifters who waited in the basement now, shivering in cages. I couldn't save them tonight. Maybe if I survive.

A flurry of activity in the wings, and a short bald man in a tux strides onstage, clutching a set of notecards. He flips through them, muttering under his breath. "Lot nine, special goods. She-wolf, trained, untouched. Unblooded." He glances at me, assessing. I might as well be a piece of meat.

I take a deep breath and get into character. Meek, submissive she-wolf trained to be a vampire's companion.

Frangelico won't be able to resist you, Xavier told me as he fastened a white collar around my neck. *You're beautiful.* It wasn't a compliment. In my world, beauty is a weapon. A weapon I was trained to use.

A stage hand hands the man in the tux a microphone.

"It's time," the auctioneer says and flaps his hand at me. I take a deep breath, raise my head, and glide barefoot onto the stage.

Lucius

"Sire, so good of you to join us." A bowing vampire greets me as I step out of my limo. My bodyguards block his way until I motion them to step aside.

"I was told this is the place to buy a shifter." I survey the rundown building, the empty marquee.

"Yes, yes, you are correct." Dante gives a little laugh and runs to get the door. "The first half of the auction is over, but the remaining lots are sublime, I'm told. The *creme de la creme*. This way, please…"

I stride past the obsequious vampire, wondering why I ever turned him. All my sired eventually disappoint. It's my curse.

Groups of well-dressed vampires discreetly watch me pass. I didn't expect to slip in unnoticed, but the way Dante keeps bobbing alongside me and babbling, I might as well have a spotlight shining on me.

The theater is old, but holds its own charm. A glass chandelier glows above my head. The red stage curtains have been brushed recently. But not even the strong cologne and perfume worn by the vampire audience can completely cover the scent of shifter fur and fear.

I've been told the shifters are willing. Desperate for a protector, they agree to be sold to a vampire with a taste for shifter blood. There certainly are enough of us willing to pay good money for a pet.

"As you can see, our renovations have only begun. We've worked to preserve the integrity of the 1920s archi-tecture—" Dante stops his tour abruptly when I lower myself into an aisle seat.

"Sire," he says, his hands fluttering in front of him. "We've prepared a seat for you in the middle of the aisle. This row has not been replaced—"

"It is fine," I nod to my protective detail and they take up stations around the aisle I've chosen. Six of the best bodyguards money can buy, their weapons hidden under their suits. They're the guards people can see. I have more layers of protection than anyone can guess. After a thousand years of assassination attempts, one learns to plan ahead.

Dante hovers close, still trying to get me to move to a larger, newer seat. "These old seats have springs that aren't very comfortable."

He's right, one spring is digging into my backside at this very moment.

"I prefer this seat," I say and turn my attention to the empty stage.

Dust motes dance in the too bright spotlights. The curtains ripple and the room fills with the audiences' expectant murmur.

I stretch out my legs and ignore Dante's nervous hand fluttering. The fact that the vampire wants me to move hasn't escaped my notice. He keeps turning and signaling someone in the balcony.

My sired are plotting something. From the pains they took to stage this auction, their plot has been in the works for some time.

No matter. In my long lifetime, I've found one coup is much like another.

Theophilus, one of my sired, takes a seat a few rows ahead of me. He turns and bows his head. I tip my own in acknowledgement, and beckon him over.

"Sire," he says when he reaches my side, and bows. "How may I be of service?"

"How many auctions have been held here?"

He glances around the dimly lit room. "A fair amount.

I only heard of them a few months ago. This is my third time."

"And the shifters are willing?"

"As willing as they can be." He grimaces. "Most are rare species. Without a large clan to protect them, they fall prey to stronger shifters."

"So they agree to this?" I wave a hand at the stage. "Is it really better to belong to a vampire?"

"I am not a shifter, so I would not know. My guess is a life in servitude is better than no life at all."

I press my lips together. Most shifters I've met would rather be free. After all, they are part wild animal.

"Do you have any further questions about the auction?" Theophilus asks. Of all my sired, he's the least likely to conspire against me, but that doesn't mean he hasn't.

"Not at this time."

"Do you intend to bid, Sire?"

I study Theophilus' face for a hint of emotion. Interest, hope, anything. "I haven't decided." I give him an enigmatic smile.

"You might be surprised. Many of these shifters are naturally submissive. Owning such a powerful creature can be exhilarating."

"That is something to consider," I murmur.

"When you live forever, there are so few new pleasures to enjoy." Theophilus glances at the stage and licks his lips. A blatant show of anticipation.

Perhaps there is nothing nefarious about these auctions. In the long life of a vampire, it's easy to succumb to boredom. Boredom begets deeper and deeper perversions.

"When you live as long as I have, there are no new pleasures," I say. "You make do with the old."

Theophilus bows his head. "With all due respect, consider bidding tonight. Some of the shifters agree to the auction, but put up delicious resistance after they're bought. Subduing them provides months of entertainment, if you draw it out."

"Months? You surprise me, Theophilus," I drawl, baiting him. "With patience, an expert can enjoy a victim for years."

He flushes. "These shifters will not last years. You can't turn them, after all."

"As you say," I pretend to agree. "I suppose the shine wears off after a few weeks. Months, if the victim is special."

"Shifters are stronger than humans, but no one can withstand a vampire. They all break, in the end."

"Yes," I turn my attention back to the stage. "Everyone breaks in the end." Even vampires.

Minutes pass and I pretend not to notice the audience members studying me. I steeple my fingers. Tonight I will sit through the auction, feigning interest. In a month I will host a party with a select number of my lieutenants. By then I'll know which of my sired plotted against me. I already have an idea.

"Ladies and gentlemen, please take your seats. The final part of the auction is about to begin."

The house lights go down and a ripple of anticipation runs around the room. The curtain parts.

And she appears.

~

Selene

"Lot nine, special goods," the auctioneer announces.

I stand on the small platform, staring into an ocean of white light. The spotlights blind me before I remember to lower my gaze to the floor. I'm supposed to be submissive. A perfect little pet for a vampire.

"Female, wolf shifter, twenty-two. She has been trained in the submissive arts but..." the auctioneer pauses and lowers his voice. "She's never been blooded. Never been mounted either. That's right ladies and gentle vampires... she's a virgin."

Do I imagine an excited murmur in the rows beyond the lights? My training kicks in and smooths my features before my lip curls in disgust.

"Turn around, sweetheart, give us a show," the auctioneer orders.

I pivot dutifully, returning to my resting stance. I bow my head a little.

"Bidding starts at one hundred thousand," the auctioneer calls. "One hundred thousand for this pure, untouched virgin. Do I have one hundred—yes, there in the back. Gentleman in the red bowtie. Anyone else want to own this fine specimen of shifter beauty? Can I get two —" The bidding goes higher, spurred by the auctioneer's excited prattle. I squint into the lights, but I can't see a thing. How many people are in the audience? Ten? Twenty? A hundred? Somewhere, perhaps in the balcony, Xavier is watching.

It doesn't matter. I'm only here for one vampire, and

one alone. Lucius Frangelico. I need to capture his interest.

I drop my gaze to the stage and try to look meek. What will entice a vampire king to bid on me? I lick my red lips, but can't bring myself to take a sultry pose. Not when I want to punch someone for subjecting shifters to this disgusting event.

My fists itch to clench. I force my shoulders to relax.

This will be over soon.

Lucius

She's not submissive. That's my first impression of the beautiful she-wolf. She glares at the floor in front of her bare feet. Whenever the auctioneer mentions her virginal status, the corner of her mouth twitches. They dressed her in a soft bit of nothing, a garment closer to a negligee than evening wear. Something silky that begs to be ripped off. She has bruises on her arms—a sign she's been manhandled—but nothing about her is fragile. She's tall, tempting, an amazon with a crown of white gold hair.

Something about her is familiar. She raises her head and shoots a glare into every corner of the theater, and the memory is lost. My body responds, blood rushing to my groin. What would it be like to own such a creature? To tame and master her?

I school my expression into one of boredom. The she-wolf tempts me, that's all. Something new and amusing to divert my attention for a time. Immortality reduces every-thing—pleasure and pain—into a temporary diversion. But this she-wolf might make me forget that for a little while.

On top of that, she looks like someone I once knew...

On stage, she licks her painted lips. My slacks grow tighter and my hands knot into fists. My bidding number rests on the floor next to my shoe. Dante must have left it there.

I won't bid tonight. But it is so tempting.

In the row in front of me, Theophilus clears his throat. "See what I mean, Sire?"

"Yes," I say, leaning forward to study the she-wolf again. "I do."

Selene

"Five hunret, five hunret, can I get five hunret—" the auctioneer bleats as the auction runs out of steam. He pauses and scratches his chin. "No? Perhaps you need more incentive."

He waves to someone offstage and three beefy stage-hands march straight towards me.

"What?" I mouth to the auctioneer, but he just looks smug. The first man reaches me and tugs at my dresses' strap.

"Time to get naked, sweetheart."

My hand flies up before I can stop it. I push Mouth-breather Number One away from me just as his two buddies arrive and clamp down on my arms, right on top of the bruises Xavier left.

"Bitch," Number One mutters. His beefy hand grabs the straps crossing over my back and tears them away. The garment sags, baring my breasts right as I get one arm free.

My training kicks in. I lean left and kick the man on my right in the crotch. He goes down and I jerk, bringing the man on my left off balance. I smash my fist into his face and flip him over my back. He crashes into Number One. I crouch in a fighter's stance in the center of three downed thugs.

The auctioneer is laughing.

"Ladies and gentlemen, can I get a round of applause for lot nine?" A smattering of golf claps fills the theater. My cheeks heat. I didn't defend myself as part of some fucking act.

Except it was. Around me, the thugs stir and get to their feet. The auctioneer waves them off and they slouch away.

"Show's over, folks," the auctioneer announces. "Who wants to go home with her tonight? Bidding starts at five hundred thousand."

My dress is tangled around my hips. I shove it off and kick it away.

"We've got a live one! Feisty. Will you be enough to master her? Five hundred and you'll find out."

Lucius

The she-wolf stands naked on stage, her chest heaving. Gone is any semblance of meek servitude. A lock of hair falls out of her braid and she tucks it impatiently away, glaring at everything and nothing.

She is magnificent. If I owned her, the fun I would

have while we fought each other for dominance every night.

Unfortunately, I'm not the only one who thinks this.

"Damn," Theophilus breathes. The next time the auctioneer calls for a bid, he raises his paddle.

I see red.

"Theophilus," I growl, putting enough compulsion in my voice to make his head snap around. I hold out my hand, palm up. "Give it to me."

He obeys, but all around me, vampires are bidding for the she-wolf. She stands in a pool of light, not even trying to hide her disgust. What made her agree to be auctioned? She doesn't seem the type.

I beckon to Theophilus. "These shifters. If someone bids on them, do they get a portion of the money?"

Understanding lights his eyes. "No. They'll become your property. They don't come with anything. But their family might be compensated."

That matched the information I was given about the shifter slavers. These men, typically rogue shifters, found hidden shifter clans and offered money for the most submissive in the pack. Threats were also most likely involved. I couldn't see this she-wolf allowing herself to be a part of that bargain. But perhaps she agreed if the money went to her family.

I sat back as the bids raged around me. A mystery. I'm becoming more intrigued by the second.

"One million," someone calls a bid. I turn and look across the aisle. A large vampire wearing an eyepatch looks back at me. Only a lifetime of controlling my emotions keeps me from showing my surprise.

Xavier. What's he doing here? I haven't seen him for decades. Maybe a century. He inclines his head in mocking acknowledgement. The last time we met, we were enemies.

There's quiet as the auctioneer and audience absorb his bid. Onstage, the she-wolf trembles as if she remembers why she's here.

And I remember who the wolf reminds me of. Her face becomes another, a waifish imp with a cloud of white gold hair. My first vampire lover. The only woman, perhaps, I ever loved. Georgianna.

Xavier's fangs glint at me from across the aisle. He never forgave me for taking Georgianna from him, and now, it seemed, he would snatch this wolf right from under my nose.

This one's mine, his gloating face seems to say. Poor she-wolf. Xavier always broke his toys. If not for fun, then to prevent anyone else from enjoying them.

My fingers clench on the bidding paddle. This whole auction, Xavier's appearance, the she-wolf who looks like Georgianna's ghost come to life—it's a ploy. A set up. It has to be. It's too convenient.

Somebody's up to something. If my sired have thrown their lots in with Xavier, then they have rebelled past the point of forgiveness. Their lives are over.

But if all of this is Xavier acting alone, then it might be interesting to play the game. Save the she-wolf. Parade her before my court, and draw Xavier into my net.

What is the human saying? Keep your friends close… and your enemies closer.

Oh yes. These next few weeks will be very entertaining. I lean back in my seat and raise my paddle.

~

Selene

"One million."

Blood rushes to my head. That was Xavier's voice. He's bidding on me? Why?

I clench my hands in front of me, controlling my shudder. Have I failed? I can't fail. There's nothing left for me but the road ahead. The mission to entice Frangelico.

The silence stretches on and my nerves are screaming. Xavier doesn't like failure. That's a lesson I've learned over and over again. Pain is a great teacher. I'm strong enough to withstand it, but if I fail at this, I don't know—

A deep voice breaks the stillness. "Ten million."

A hush falls over the entire theater, every creature, me included, holding our breath.

The auctioneer looks like he can't believe his luck. "T-ten million." He mops his forehead and glances around the theater, biting his lip. I wait for him to raise the bid, but it seems jumping so high so quickly is enough to make an auctioneer tongue-tied. At last he raps his gavel and shouts. "Sold! To the gentleman with the deepest pockets. Vampire King Lucius Frangelico."

There's a ringing in my ears. I stoop and gather up the pieces of the ripped dress. It worked. It worked. He bought me.

In a few minutes I'll be in the clutches of my new

vampire master. Everything is going as planned.

The curtain sweeps across the stage, and I'm left blinking in the dark.

The auctioneer announces something about a break and walks off stage. Once he's in the wings, he beckons me to follow.

"Good girl," he tells me, rubbing his hands together. Probably imagining holding ten million dollars in his fat grubby fingers. I close my eyes, dizzy. What sort of vampire pays ten million for a wolf pet? What will he do with me?

It doesn't matter. It will all be over soon. Any bit of unpleasantness in the meantime, well, I've been trained to take a lot of pain.

Four guards march up and surround me. They don't touch me, so I don't make a fuss. Beyond them, the thugs who manhandled me lurk in the murky shadows. One has an ice pack to his face. The one whose crotch I hit is gone. The last one glowers at me, but dooen't get close. They won't dare touch me now. I belong to the Vampire King. The thought hits me like a blow and makes me sway on my feet.

A young, slender man appears at my elbow. I turn and avert my eyes when I catch his scent. Not human. Vampire.

"His Majesty would like you to put this on." The young man holds up a suit jacket for me to slip into. I hand off my ripped dress to a guard and let the oversized jacket envelop me. The sleeves hang over my wrists and cover my legs to mid thigh. I've worn dresses that are less modest. I wore one tonight.

"His Majesty will collect you soon. Do you need anything? Food, some water?"

Shoes would be nice, but I shake my head. I tuck my face into the collar of the jacket and inhale the subtle, expensive cologne clinging to the fabric. The cologne doesn't hide the familiar cold stone scent. This jacket was recently worn by a vampire.

"This way," the auctioneer leads us into the green room. The young-looking vampire wrinkles his nose.

"Do you expect the king to come back here? It's a dump." When the auctioneer grovels and denies that he would ever wish the great Frangelico to sully his shoes by stepping into this room, the young vampire growls, "Then find us a better place to wait. This is the king's property." He waves a hand at me. "The respect you show her is the respect you show the king."

That's how we end up in another room, smelling of fresh paint and filled with new furniture. It's upstairs. The young vampire fusses over me, finding me a bottle of water, and bemoaning my lack of shoes.

I tune everything out. Nothing matters until I meet Frangelico.

My new master.

No. He will never own me. He will think I belong to him. By the time he learns the truth, it will be too late.

I face the door and wait for the target to enter. Lucius Frangelico, the face that haunts me. The source of all my nightmares. The vampire who killed my pack, made me an orphan. If it wasn't for Xavier, I'd be dead. I owe him everything. And the debt will never be repaid. Xavier gave me life, but he also gave me a reason to live. Years of training and planning, culminating in a single mission: revenge.

And now I've been sold to the Vampire King. I will infiltrate his private home, let him bring me to his sleeping lair. Earn his trust. Wait until the moment is right.

All my life I've been waiting for this. All my training, all my hard work for one goal.

I'm going to kill Lucius Frangelico.

Alpha's Blood: Coming April 18th

I bought her. I own her. But she'll never be mine…
** *A Vampire King…***

The moment she stepped on stage, I had to have her in my bed. My submissive, kneeling at my feet.

But this captive virgin is more than what she seems…

A spy in my kingdom. A weapon honed by my enemy. She hates me, but hate is a passion perilously close to love...

** *A captured queen…***

All my life I've trained for one purpose. One ultimate goal: kill the Vampire King.

I expected a fight. Pain. Torture. I didn't expect to want him. My body is a weapon he turns against me.

But I can't forget my fallen pack. My quest for revenge. My mission is simple:

Seduce him. Earn his trust. Bring him down.

Above all: don't fall in love.

Read Now

READ ALL THE BAD BOY ALPHA BOOKS

Bad Boy Alphas Series

Alpha's Temptation

Alpha's Danger

Alpha's Prize

Alpha's Challenge

Alpha's Obsession

Alpha's Desire

Alpha's War

Alpha's Mission

Alpha's Bane

Alpha's Secret

Alpha's Prey

Alpha's Blood

Alpha's Sun

Shifter Ops

Alpha's Moon

Alpha's Vow

Alpha's Revenge

READ ALL THE BAD BOY ALPHA BOOKS

Alpha's Fire
Alpha's Rescue

Midnight Doms
Alpha's Blood
His Captive Mortal
All Soul's Night
Additional books by other authors

WANT FREE BOOKS?

-Go to http://subscribepage.com/alphastemp to sign up for Renee Rose's newsletter and receive a free copy of *Alpha's Temptation, Theirs to Protect, Owned by the Marine, Theirs to Punish, The Alpha's Punishment, Disobedience at the Dressmaker's* and *Her Billionaire Boss.* In addition to the free stories, you will also get special pricing, exclusive previews and news of new releases.

-Go to www.leesavino.com to sign up for Lee Savino's awesomesauce mailing list and get a FREE Berserker book —too hot to publish anywhere else!

OTHER TITLES BY RENEE ROSE

Chicago Bratva

"Prelude" in Black Light: Roulette War

The Director

The Fixer

"Owned" in Black Light: Roulette Rematch

The Enforcer

The Soldier

The Hacker

The Bookie

The Cleaner

Vegas Underground Mafia Romance

King of Diamonds

Mafia Daddy

Jack of Spades

Ace of Hearts

Joker's Wild

His Queen of Clubs

Dead Man's Hand

Wild Card

Contemporary

Daddy Rules Series

Fire Daddy

Hollywood Daddy

Stepbrother Daddy

Master Me Series

Her Royal Master

Her Russian Master

Her Marine Master

Yes, Doctor

Double Doms Series

Theirs to Punish

Theirs to Protect

Holiday Feel-Good

Scoring with Santa

Saved

Other Contemporary

Black Light: Valentine Roulette

Black Light: Roulette Redux

Black Light: Celebrity Roulette

Black Light: Roulette War

Black Light: Roulette Rematch

Punishing Portia (written as Darling Adams)

The Professor's Girl

Safe in his Arms

Paranormal

Two Marks Series

Untamed

Tempted

Desired

Enticed

Wolf Ranch Series

Rough

Wild

Feral

Savage

Fierce

Ruthless

Wolf Ridge High Series

Alpha Bully

Alpha Knight

Bad Boy Alphas Series

Alpha's Temptation

Alpha's Danger

Her Alien Masters

ALSO BY LEE SAVINO

Paranormal romance

The Berserker Saga and Berserker Brides (menage werewolves)

These fierce warriors will stop at nothing to claim their mates.

Draekons (Dragons in Exile) with Lili Zander (menage alien dragons)

Crashed spaceship. Prison planet. Two big, hulking, bronzed aliens who turn into dragons. The best part? The dragons insist I'm their mate.

Bad Boy Alphas with Renee Rose (bad boy werewolves)

Never ever date a werewolf.

Tsenturion Masters with Golden Angel

Who knew my e-reader was a portal to another galaxy? Now I'm stuck with a fierce alien commander who wants to claim me as his own.

Contemporary Romance

Royal Bad Boy

I'm not falling in love with my arrogant, annoying, sex god boss. Nope. No way.

Royally Fake Fiancé

The Duke of New Arcadia has an image problem only a fiancé can fix. And I'm the lucky lady he's chosen to play Cinderella.

Beauty & The Lumberjacks

After this logging season, I'm giving up sex. For…reasons.

Her Marine Daddy

My hot Marine hero wants me to call him daddy…

Her Dueling Daddies

Two daddies are better than one.

Innocence: dark mafia romance with Stasia Black

I'm the king of the criminal underworld. I always get what I want. And she is my obsession.

Beauty's Beast: a dark romance with Stasia Black

Years ago, Daphne's father stole from me. Now it's time for her to pay her family's debt…with her body.

ABOUT RENEE ROSE

USA TODAY BESTSELLING AUTHOR RENEE ROSE loves a dominant, dirty-talking alpha hero! She's sold over two million copies of steamy romance with varying levels of kink. Her books have been featured in USA Today's *Happily Ever After* and *Popsugar*. Named Eroticon USA's Next Top Erotic Author in 2013, she has also won *Spunky and Sassy's* Favorite Sci-Fi and Anthology author, *The Romance Reviews* Best Historical Romance, and has hit the *USA Today* bestseller list over a dozen times with her Shifter Ops, Chicago Bratva, and Wolf Ranch series, as well as various anthologies.

.

Please follow her on:
Bookbub | Goodreads

Renee loves to connect with readers!
www.reneeroseromance.com
reneeroseauthor@gmail.com

ABOUT LEE SAVINO

Lee Savino is a USA today bestselling author, mom and chocoholic.

Warning: Do not read her Berserker series, or you will be addicted to the huge, dominant warriors who will stop at nothing to claim their mates.

I repeat: Do. Not. Read. The Berserker Saga. Particularly not the thrilling excerpt below.

Download a free book from www.leesavino.com (don't read that either. Too much hot, sexy lovin').

Printed in Great Britain
by Amazon